CONTENTS

I0621864

Darkness Forged: Eschaton Cycle
Legends of the Ragnarok Era Book 1
MATT LARKIN
Editors: Fred Roth and Brenda J. Pierson
Cover: Yocla Designs

Copyright © 2017 Matt Larkin.

Incandescent Phoenix Books
mattlarkinbooks.com

MIDGARD

THULE

NIDAVELLIR

SVIARLAND

LAPPMARKEN

JAMTLA

DALAR

NJARAR

UPSAL

OSTERGOTLAND

SKANE

MORIMARUSA

NORREYYSKE

CIMBRIA

LANDVIK SEA

ARUS SJAELLAND

BURGUNDAHOLMR

BRETLAND

REIDGOTALAND

LAALAND

RIJNLAND

MENZLIN

XANTEN

HUNALAND

BAIA

SWABIA

STYRIA

VALLAND

AQUISGRANA

IDAVOLLIR

OUTER MIKLAGARD

ANDALUS

KARJUBA

MIDDLE SEA

VANAHEIM

SERKLAND CALIPHATE

POHJOLA
KVENLAND
KALEVALA
SAMODIYTSIA
UTGARD
BJARMALAND
MIDGARD WALL
HOLMGARD
QAZAN
JARNVID
HALFHAUGR
AUJUM
KIOVIA
TARAZ
HYRCANIAN SEA
BLACK SEA
MIKLAGARD
MIKLAGARD

EXTRA RESOURCES

For full color, higher-res maps, character lists, location
overviews, and glossaries, check out the bonus resources
here:
https://tinyurl.com/y47j3gcj

Join the Skalds' Tribe newsletter and get access to exclusive insider information and your FREE copy of *The Moments of Kadmus.*

https://www.mattlarkinbooks.com/skalds/

PART I

Year 97, Age of Vinegthor
End of Summer

1

VOLUND

*O*f the many works Volund had wrought in his life, the house at Wolf Lake always filled him with the most pride. He had not forged it in shadow nor worked into it any ancient dverg craft—save for a few runes of warding carved between the boards. No, nine winters back, he and his half-brothers had cut fresh timber and built the house on the lake shore as refuge from a broken world. And every time he returned home after a long hunt such as this, that first sight of the roof's peak filled him with more satisfaction, more contentment, than any other place he had known.

"Volund has that look on his face again," Slagfid said, or panted, rather. Volund's eldest brother had a reindeer slung over his shoulders. Even with his impressive build, they had to take turns carrying this catch. The beast was damned heavy.

Agilaz nodded sternly. He did most everything sternly, but Volund didn't hold it against him—much. It was Agilaz's steady aim that had brought down their prey, as usual. "I'm also eager to see my wife."

Slagfid chuckled. "See her? Or enter her?"

Agilaz scowled and Volund tried not to smile. He waved his torch around, dispelling the mist. It was growing thicker as evening drew nigh. The torch's flame would protect them in daylight, but it would be best they sat round a real fire before sunset. Such mists covered all of Midgard and were apt to poison men's minds and bodies both.

"Oh, come now," Slagfid said. "Don't tell me you aren't keen to pry apart those magnificent thighs of hers, brother. I know I am."

Their middle brother spun and shoved him, sending man and deer collapsing into a heap in the snow. Slagfid, however, just continued laughing. "I meant *my* wife, brother. Not yours."

Volund snorted as he helped Slagfid up. Somehow, he suspected Slagfid had said *exactly* what he meant, just to get under Agilaz's skin. They each treasured their wives, without any doubt. Notwithstanding that Slagfid had suggested—once or twice—they might trade wives for a night. For her part, Volund's wife, Altvir, did not seem the least bit offended, but Agilaz would never have agreed to share Olrun with anyone.

Nor, in truth, could Volund stand to be parted from Altvir. She brought out the best in him. Or held down the worst. He was never quite certain.

Agilaz paused now, staring at their house in the valley. Volund followed his gaze. The wall's gate was closed, but from up here he could see the house's door stood wide open. An odd sight. Even if the women had gone down to the lake to bathe—and they did so no matter how cold the weather grew—they ought not to have left the door ajar. That might risk allowing the fire to go out, something no one in the North Realms would dare allow.

Volund shared a glance with Agilaz. As one, they took off running, snow crunching under their heels, paying no mind to Slagfid's shouts from behind. Wolf Lake earned its name for the dire wolves that prowled the woods throughout this valley. Such animals should not prove a threat to their wives—valkyries all, and master warriors. Should not, and yet, on occasion, a varulf or two had taken to running with the packs. Mostly, the brothers chased them off. Once, though, a stubborn werewolf had forced them to hunt him down.

Not bothering with the gate, Volund vaulted over the wall and dashed into the house. An instant later, Agilaz shoved him aside. The place showed no sign of disturbance. The bed alcoves were neat, still lined with furs. The pots hung from the walls. The fire still crackled in the pit at the house's heart. But there was no sign of ...

Agilaz pushed forward and knelt by the fire pit, hand shaking as he reached for something.

Before Volund could see what it was, Slagfid plowed his way inside. "What in Hel's icy trench has gotten into you two?"

"Olrun ..." Agilaz said.

And as Volund turned his back, he saw. Agilaz held his wife's ring between two fingers. Its rosy, golden hue glittered in the firelight. They *always* wore those rings, even when bathing. Altvir had told him once, when they were first wed, that the ring was a symbol of her oath—her vow to some Etheric being beyond life and death, an entity she spoke of in whispers, if at all. And Volund had told her that same ring would now serve as their oath in marriage.

Two more rings glittered around the fire pit. Volund fell to his knees. His hand shook as he reached for the one Altvir had worn. His fingers hesitated a hairsbreadth away.

This simple object whispered to him, like the hiss of a serpent, as shadows began to gather at the edges of the house. Just the sun setting. But as the darkness lengthened, it danced. It hungered.

It was starting again.

Was it urd—the very will of Fate?

Or was his mind playing tricks on him in his fear?

Volund snatched the ring. It had grown warm by the fire, so warm he could almost imagine it still graced Altvir's slim finger. And that warmth banished the shadows. They crept away, seeping back into the corners of the house like the mist, fleeing a torch. And the ring pulsed like a beating heart. Her heart, calling to him.

His brothers were there, but he had lost track of them. All he heard, all he saw, was that pulsing ring resting in his palm. And it demanded his utter devotion. As she had. Small, sized for a woman. Uncertain why he did so, he slipped it onto his little finger and clenched his fist.

A welcome calmness settled over him, and only then did he realize his entire chest had been trembling. He clenched his fist, pressing it over his heart. That pulsing was still throbbing through him, blurring his vision, lulling his mind. Beating.

Summoning.

Volund fell to his side, overcome by something that was not sight. Not exactly. And yet his heart and soul saw. A battleground, men dying in wars. They fought one another. They *always* did, despite the mists of Niflheim choking the mortal world, despite the Otherworldly dangers that lurked in those mists. Still, the dying kingdoms fought for the scraps of a dying land. It was half the reason the brothers had settled here, beyond the bounds of civilization, separated from the world of men.

And their wives had gone back to it. The ring told him. Almost, if he listened hard enough, he could hear the screams of the dying over that ever-present heartbeat. Men were always dying, and as a valkyrie, Altvir had once delivered their souls unto the Realms beyond Midgard. No matter how oft he asked of the Otherworlds, she would not speak of them.

The night breeze battered his face. She was flying. Had taken the form of a swan and flown away.

Left him.

Why?

Why, after nine winters, would she abandon her home? Why would she do this?

"Papa?"

Volund shook himself, trying to regain his vision. It came back slowly, the house seeming to warp and spin even as he shook. She was gone. She was gone! Those shadows were laughing at him, mocking. Growing bold and creeping out of their hiding holes, sliding ever closer. And yet also on the periphery, never there if he looked directly. They were coming for him.

A child was crying. Groaning, Volund crawled to the threshold. Outside the house, Agilaz cradled his son in his arms. Hermod had five winters now. Had he been outside? In the *night*? Frey's flaming sword. He must have wandered out, seeking his mother.

Slagfid lay on the floor, clutching his wife's ring as Volund himself had done. As Agilaz had probably just recovered from.

A terrible heat built in his chest. And with that heat came the rage. He wanted to punish someone for this. It was *someone's* fault. It had to be. Slagfid. Maybe his own wife, Svanhit, had tired of Slagfid's not-so-subtle hints they ought to trade wives. Was that it? Had she convinced her sister valkyries to flee because of him?

Damn him. Damn the lustful, arrogant fool. Volund seized his half-brother and heaved him to his feet. Slagfid shook himself, glazed eyes starting to clear. Volund punched him in the face. Slagfid pitched backward, almost falling into the fire pit.

"You did this, didn't you?" He could push him into the flames, immolate the one who had ruined their lives.

An instant later Agilaz wrapped him in a bear hug, pinning his arms to his side. Volund strained, slowly breaking his older brother's grip. Agilaz might have been strong, but Volund had spent years slaving at a dverg forge. His muscles had become like the rocks from which the dvergar crawled.

"Volund!" Agilaz shouted.

Slagfid regained his feet, inspecting his bloody lip with a hand. He spat. "Yes, little brother. After nine winters I decided to drive away my wife. And yours too, for good measure. All while hunting reindeer at your side. By the way, while you slept, I also fucked the goddess Freyja. And slew a dragon. At the same time. Gods you should have seen it, what a tale to be told from that."

"Shut up!" Volund broke Agilaz's grip but did not go after Slagfid again, despite the roiling hunger in his gut to hit him, to punish him for his words and arrogance and for *this*—this nightmare.

"They've gone," Agilaz said.

Volund spun on him. "Any other obvious wisdom you want to share?"

Agilaz glowered. "They have gone to fulfill oaths made long ago to some ancient power. Perhaps a fresh war draws them, perhaps they can no longer deny the pull of their vows."

"And what?" Volund folded his arms. "That's it? You'll leave your son without a mother?"

Leave yourself, leave them all, without their wives. Without Altvir. She was the sun shining in the sky, banishing the shadows. He ran his thumb over the ring, drawing small comfort from its grooves, its intricate etching.

"No." Agilaz shook his head and held up his hand, displaying the ring. He too wore it on his little finger. "I'm going to find her. With this. I can feel Olrun. I know she still loves me. Maybe she could not break her oath to whatever god or goddess she serves. But she left this for me, and I have to believe it a sign she still wants to hold her oath to me, as well. That she wants me to follow, to find her. And so I will."

"How will you know where to look?" Slagfid asked.

Agilaz shut his eyes and clenched his fist around the ring. "I can feel her. To the southeast."

"Southeast? You mean Aujum. Those are the lands of Ás tribes." Slagfid said.

Agilaz nodded. "Then little surprise there is war."

Volund shut his eyes and concentrated on Altvir. Yes. She was there, somewhere close. North? Did he need to travel north? Everything was a confusing rush of sensations. Like a dream, nonsensical if viewed apart from its own reality. But in that dream ... in the dream, she seemed to have gone north.

He opened his mouth to say so, but Slagfid spoke first. "I must go south, then. Southwest, I think."

"The islands?" Agilaz frowned. For once, his stern look was justified. There were powers on those islands even dvergar were not keen to challenge. Powers of ancient times, best left sleeping, best left forgotten. Some said, there, the Old Kingdoms had not entirely died out.

"They have flown in three different directions," Volund said.

Slagfid shrugged. "Perhaps war spreads throughout all the North Realms. What say you then? We must go our separate ways and meet back here once we have reclaimed our wives. Either way, let us agree to meet here again, in one year."

Volund shuddered. The valley had been a refuge. In nine winters he had barely left, and never without Altvir at his side. But without her, even this refuge would become hollow, empty, save for the ever-lengthening shadows grasping at his mind.

The ring pulsed. A heartbeat, calling to his own. He might remain here, wait, and pray to all the gods she returned to him. But perhaps Agilaz was right. Perhaps the valkyries wanted their husbands to come after them. And if such was the price to reclaim his wife, he would do so. He would trek across Midgard and even beyond if needs be.

But on his soul, he was going to find Altvir.

That was *his* oath.

2

SLAGFID

*N*umerous isles dotted the Morimarusa, many of them claimed by jarls or petty kings who strove to dominate those jarls. None of those so-called kingdoms concerned Slagfid. Only the call of the ring mattered. Rumors, though, legends even, spoke of other powers calling some few islands in Reidgotaland home. According to these stories, after their fall, one of the Old Kingdoms yet lingered, a slumbering shadow of its former self. This kingdom, the Niflungar—people steeped in knowledge even völvur feared—had retreated into mist-cloaked isles. New kingdoms rose around them, but still there remained a shroud of fear. Sometimes, men ventured to one island or another and never returned.

No one wished to take him there, especially not on the cusp of winter, so he'd been forced to row a small boat himself. His arms ached with the effort, but his ring grew ever warmer, telling him he drew nigh unto Svanhit. Probably, any two of the small kingdoms were squabbling over an island or some other stretch of land. And their battles—rather, the heroic deaths those battles engendered—would draw valkyries. Svanhit always liked a good battle. Sometimes they had sparred, Svanhit winning her fair share of their struggles.

It had bothered him, at first, a woman besting him as often as not, when almost no man had ever done so. But then, she was a valkyrie, not just any woman. Svanhit knew the ways of war well, and was an expert in sword and shield, bow and spear. Besides, their matches ended most often with them going at each other like rabbits in heat. He didn't mind that so much.

A chill sweat dripped down his back. He glanced over his shoulder. Yes, there in the distance was an island, maybe the source of the battles. Certainly he felt the warmth of his ring increasing. The sky above that island though, it grew dark, a storm sweeping in. He watched it a moment longer.

By the ghosts of his ancestors, it was coming toward him. He'd never make it back to his last stop before it hit, nor could he be sure of finding land if he turned more southerly. It seemed Njord was angry with him. Probably should have made a sacrifice before he left.

"Father, if you're listening ... I need to reach land before the storm reaches me. Grant me strength."

He turned back and heaved on the oars, propelling himself with all the speed he could muster.

RAIN LASHED AGAINST HIM, whipping his hair about his face, nigh to blinding him. He'd mocked Agilaz for keeping such short hair. Seemed his half-brother had a reason for it. The waves had grown in intensity, casting his rowboat off course. The dim sensation of his ring told him that.

"Njord, if you get me through this ... I will offer up nine lives in your name. I swear it."

A surge of water crashed over his boat. One of his oars fell from his grasp, then disappeared, carried away from the boat. The Vanr did not seem to be listening. Damn fickle, the gods could be. Especially the god of wind and sea.

He pushed his hair back from his eyes. Damn it. He still couldn't make out land.

Another wave rocked his boat and flung him forward. His shoulder hit the rail, and he almost tumbled over the side.

The gods did not love him this day. And his father's ghost was not listening either.

He could not steer the boat with one oar, and the waves were tossing him about so violently it might not have mattered. The winter storms had come early. "Svanhit ... I hope you guide me true." The ring pulled him to one side, tempting him with the promise of land.

With a deep breath, he vaulted the rail and dove into the sea. He was already soaked, but still, that first plunge felt like slipping into the icy world of Hel. The deeper he dove, though, the less force the waves held. In the darkness, he could make out almost naught.

All he could do was strive forward. Trust the ring.

Men claimed serpents and mermaids and even a terrible kraken lived beneath the Morimarusa. He didn't even see any fish.

Lungs were about to burst. Slagfid broke the surface, gasping. The moment he did so, another wave crashed over him. It flung water down his throat. He sputtered, coughing up a lungful of the stuff. Please, Svanhit. Or any other god who might be listening. He did not want to die, pulled down into the net of Rán. Some said the mermaid queen spat out her rejects as sea draugar, forever haunting the sea where they died. Slagfid would not wish such an urd even upon his enemies.

He dove under again. His lungs wanted to explode in an instant. He'd not had a full breath of air, but he was not like to get one.

Yes, at this point he'd accept aid from Rán or her dire husband, Aegir. He'd almost welcome succor from Hel herself.

None of them answered.

Follow the ring.

His whole chest was on fire.

He did not want to die like this.

"He lives." A woman's voice.

Svanhit had come for him.

Slagfid blinked. A man had flung him over his shoulder, was carrying him. An armored woman trotted beside them, the wind batting her hair over her face.

Svanhit ...

"Svanhit."

He jerked awake. He lay on furs, beside a fire. A wooden house, thick with wood smoke and the smell of cooking fish.

A woman sat a few feet away, sharpening a sword. Other warriors, too, one tending to a pot over the fire.

The woman rose at his voice. She had Svanhit's height and build, her hair color. But it was not she. She knelt beside him and peered into his eyes. "I am Kelda Frothisdotter. And you are lucky to be alive. The gods must favor you."

Perhaps. It seemed Njord had answered his prayer—or accepted his offer of sacrifices.

"Who is Svanhit?" she asked.

He pushed himself to a sitting position. His muscles ached, trembled, and tried to refuse, but he was not about to meet these warriors lying down. They had removed their armor, but he was certain he'd seen it when they found him. Wealthy enough warriors, then.

And what should he tell them about Svanhit? That he had married a valkyrie and she had left him? They might think him Mist-mad. Or a liar. "I am Slagfid Wadesson, prince of Kvenland."

The woman cocked her head at that. "Then, prince, I should tell you my father is king of this island."

Rescued by a princess. That was a tale for the skalds.

His stomach rumbled, and a few of Kelda's men laughed. With a wooden bowl, one man scooped out a lump of fish from the pot, then handed Slagfid the bowl. Slagfid snatched it up and pried the flesh loose with his fingers. The heat seared him, but it was welcome. Haddock, and well-cooked. At this point, he'd have devoured it raw had they given it to him.

"Get the prince some ale," Kelda said, then served herself some fish.

They waited until he had finished eating before anyone spoke further to him.

Kelda broke the silence then. "You are a long way from Kvenland, aren't you? And yet you speak our tongue."

Slagfid nodded. Kvenland was part of the North Realms, but the Northern tongue diverged in different lands. "We had instruction from foreign tutors as children." One of many benefits of being a prince, even one who could never inherit the throne. Since his own father was a bastard—as were the brothers, all sired on different women—they lacked political importance. The king had still seen his bastard brother as an asset, however, and might have married Slagfid off to some noble's daughter, had things gone differently. Had his father not sent Volund to the accursed dvergar.

"I owe you my life, princess."

She waved her hand as if it were of no consequence.

"I made a vow to Njord if he would spare me, I would kill nine men in his name. But it was your men who pulled me from the sea, so I ask you. Tell me the names of your enemies, and I shall slay them for you."

"Are you so great a warrior to make such an offer?" A curious look had overtaken her face, and the other warriors, too, were watching him now.

"I have rarely met my equal with a sword." In truth, since attaining manhood, only Svanhit had bested him. And besides, Svanhit remained close, perhaps waiting for heroic deaths. Slagfid might fulfill his oath and find his wife with the same stroke. "If a man troubles you, princess, point me toward him." He yawned. "And I shall attend to him once I have rested."

One of the warriors chuckled. Slagfid noted his face. He expected he was going to like the man. "You would not be so quick to offer if you knew our foes."

Slagfid snorted. The looks on their faces, however ... stern as Agilaz and drawn out. Like men who knew they were soon bound for Valhalla and had accepted it, but found no joy in the knowledge.

Kelda rubbed her arms and looked around the hall. "You have heard of the Niflungar?"

Oh, by the ghosts of his ancestors. Slagfid scowled and nodded. The sorcerer kings had once been the terror of the old world, the greatest of the Old Kingdoms. According to the skalds who had instructed him in ancient lore, the Niflungar worshipped the goddess Hel, Queen of the Mists, and thus called themselves Children of the Mist.

"They have wakened," Kelda said. She looked faraway now. "They demand tribute—great hoards of gold, silver, all other value our people had gathered. We already send so much to Nidavellir, and now this emissary comes, claiming lineage from a dead kingdom? No, my father refused."

One of the men spit. All had hands on their weapons and kept looking about, as if expecting the mist to somehow permeate the wooden walls and choke the life from them.

Kelda seemed to look through him, at some ghastly memory and sight he'd rather not see. "They came in the night. We didn't know, didn't hear aught. But in the morning, we found a man dead in his house, door wide open. His wife and children gone. Just ... gone. And the fisherman— eyes frozen inside his skull, face twisted like he'd looked upon Hel herself."

"No one leaves their door open at night," Slagfid said.

"No," Kelda agreed. "But the next night it happened again. And again. So my father sent us into the wilds to hunt them. We found naught. And so we pass from one town to another. Three times, one of our own number has vanished in the night."

A chill shook him. How did a man track something like that? Maybe one as keen as Agilaz could do it, but Slagfid was a far better swordsman than woodsman. And was this truly the task the Vanr god wished of him? Slagfid had been careless in his oath.

Slagfid sighed. "I swore to Njord I would kill nine men in

his name. I swore to you I would fight your enemies. Grant me a sword, princess. And we will see about hunting these Mist children."

Another warrior scoffed. "If the king doesn't pay, Hel will have us all before the winter breaks."

Perhaps she would. Either way, Slagfid intended to return at least nine of her children to her.

3

VOLUND

*B*eyond the valley lay the seven petty kingdoms of Sviarland, each ruled by an equally petty king. The brothers had rarely had contact with any of them, save for trading with the nearest border town, usually done by Slagfid.

Volund had passed through that town a day back and traded some silver for supplies. Extra torches, especially. One could not walk the wilds without torches. The dvergar who trained him had spoken of days before the mists had seeped into Midgard, had confirmed the legends among men that those mists had come from the icy world of Hel—Niflheim. And they were poison to mortals. Not only to the body, but to the soul, to the mind. Those who breathed them deep went Mist-mad, lost themselves, and if they came back at all, they came back wrong. Once, Volund's own father, Wade, had cut the head off a man gone Mist-mad. Volund had been a boy, but he remembered those empty eyes, like the man was looking at something no one else could see.

Even the dvergar of Nidavellir avoided venturing out of

their subterranean domain when possible. And now Volund wandered through those mists. Forests covered much of Sviarland, so he would not lack for wood. If he wandered too far, though, he might run low on oil.

The ring kept drawing him northward. Into the heart of those damn kingdoms. Not places he had any desire to see. Nine winters had passed, yes, but the dvergar had long memories and held the deepest of grudges. They would hunt him for the rest of his days. Maybe beyond. Some said the dvergar could conjure the dead and force them into servitude, as did their own dire creators. An apt punishment for his crimes against them, perhaps. Volund shook his head. The more time he spent in civilization, the more chance for word to reach Nidavellir. A great mountain range separated Sviarland from Nidavellir, but mountains were no barrier to the dvergar. The Earth spirits were born of rock and stone, spawned in a world far below Midgard. Sooner or later, they would hear of him, and they would come for him. Such was the way of the World.

And yet, if he did not follow Altvir, he was already lost. His life would mean less than naught.

Just shadows.

So northward he pushed, but not on the sledge trails. In winter, dogsleds and sledges wore common paths one could follow between kingdoms. Common, if not safe. But Volund had less fear of the mists and the wilds than he did of wagging tongues, so he kept to the depths of the woods. He had no sled, but soon snowfall would necessitate skis or snowshoes. Those first snows always came this moon. He did not have much time.

Agilaz was the best woodsman and tracker among them. Volund could not match his brother's skill. Still, he had the ring to keep his course true. When he slept, it sang to him in a whisper. He could not make out the words, but the voice he knew. It was her voice, calling him, calming him. Saving him from himself.

The brisk wind tugged at his cloak, threatening to tear it loose from its clasp. At least the valkyries had not left in the heart of winter. True, it was easier to cross frozen lakes than go around them. But in winter, that chill could kill a man while he slept. And worse, thanks to the mist, those who died alone without a pyre might again rise.

Ahead, in a clearing, lay a stone hall. Volund hesitated. Shelter was good, especially with night approaching. But the obvious disrepair meant naught human laired in this place. Some such ruins were empty, safe from Mankind. Many, though, housed vaettir, beings of spirit keen to prey on Men foolish enough to draw nigh. Even those without vaettir could still harbor trolls and the like.

Still, a hall would have a fire pit. A fire pit meant safety, a chance to sleep without fear of mist. Volund knelt, watching the hall. No one emerged from it. No smoke from the chimney. That alone must confirm no people lived here, not any longer.

In the distance, a wolf howled.

Damn it. Night was fast approaching. He either had to claim this place or find somewhere and build a fire. As the sun set, the mist would thicken. And with it, vaettir would grow bolder. Darkness unleashed draugar, trolls, and ... worse. Vaettir even dvergar feared.

This place offered an unknown risk, but also his best chance.

He approached the hall in a crouch, staying low, hand on the sword hanging over his shoulder. He had crafted it himself, in the great forges of Nidavellir. Pattern-woven dverg steel—adamant, they called it—stronger than blades carried by men. Strong enough to cut down a varulf if need be. And yet, naught stirred as he approached.

The wall around the compound was nigh eight feet tall, much too tall for him to see over once he had drawn up against it. Runes marked it, but the work was sloppy. The dvergar had not built this place, though they might have taught the men who did. Remnants of one of the Old Kingdoms, perhaps. Volund jumped up and grasped the top of the wall. His fingers slipped immediately. A thick layer of ice coated it. It would make going in that way impossible.

That left only the front approach. The builders knew what they were doing in that much, at least. He edged along the wall, cringing at each crunch of pine needles beneath his heels. The gate had long since rotted away. Slipping his sword free, he peered around the wall's edge. The stone hall lay beyond, its entrance off-center so one could not charge straight from the gate to the door. From here he could see that the door, too, had fallen away.

Volund slipped around the wall's edge and crept nigh to the entrance. Still naught to see. The sky grew darker with each passing moment. He had no choice now. It was too late to search for other shelter.

More runes marked the hall proper, though they had faded. Perhaps they still offered some protection, barring the house against vaettir. Hard to say for certain. Had he more time, he might strengthen those runes, but not now, not tonight. Torch in one hand, sword in the other, he stepped inside. The shadows retreated at the light as though they resented it, and, almost, he swore they hissed at him. The main hall was open, not unlike a modern longhouse. On the far side, a wall separated the main hall from back rooms, so the keeper had once had enough wealth to want to hide it. If luck held, maybe he would even find a treasure hoard. More importantly though, in the center was a stone fire pit. Volund drew closer. No kindling, of course. The last of the Old Kingdoms had fallen some eight hundred years back. If this was such a ruin, of course naught would remain.

A long, low growl from behind set the hair on the back of his neck on end. He turned slowly to see a mound of fur lurching from the shadows on the far side of the hall. It lumbered forward, its gait uneven, its form massive, five, maybe six feet tall at the shoulder. A cave bear. A fucking cave bear had chosen this place to hibernate, and he'd awakened it. Thing had to weigh half a ton. And it was coming closer, moving faster with each step.

Volund backed away slowly, torch held out before him. If the bear feared it, it might well count for more than his sword. He ought to have trusted his first instinct and passed this place by. The bear snarled again.

Heart pounding, Volund's vision narrowed. Those shadows grew thicker, enclosing the bear until he could see naught else. Yes. If he slew the bear he'd have meat. A lot of meat. Yes. It had chosen its home poorly.

"Well, then," he said, "come on."

The bear growled once more, then barreled forward. Fast. Volund thrust the torch at it and dove to the side in the same motion, even as it swiped with its claws. Those dagger-like weapons scraped stone, shrieking. The torch caught the bear's foreleg, and it roared in pain.

Volund came up from his roll and thrust the torch again, barely warding off the enraged animal. It did not like fire, but that wasn't going to keep it at bay for long. It reared up on its hind legs. Volund flung himself to the ground, rolling away as fast as he could. In an instant the bear had closed the distance and swiped again. This time, he flung the torch in its face. The cave bear howled, pawing at its singed maw. Instead of retreating, Volund leapt forward and swung his sword with both hands. The adamant sliced through muscle and bone, severing the bear's foreleg at the joint. Off balance, it pitched forward.

This time, he did leap backward, immediately running for the far side of the room. A wound like that and the bear would bleed to death. Eventually. The cave bear bellowed, half running, half falling forward at a more uneven gait, driven mad with rage.

It was going to rip him to shreds before it died. He dashed into one of those back rooms and froze for a moment at what he saw. A forge—an ancient forge, long cold. It was naught compared to the smithies in Nidavellir where he had trained, and yet ... it called to him.

He shook himself and backed away from the door. Almost immediately the bear slammed into the doorway and began to wedge itself through. Had it not bulked up for the winter, it would have fit through all the quicker. But that would buy him only a moment. The forge had a back door. He could retreat that way. He could.

Instead, the bear's rage seemed to seep into him. It licked at his mind and soul, drew him forward. With a cry, he rushed forward and hacked straight down with his blade. It cleaved through the bear's skull and muzzle and stuck, held fast by the bone. The bear dropped to the floor, yanking the sword from his grasp.

His muscles trembled. It was dead. And still, he saw naught but that bear, surrounded in darkness. Calling him. With a foot planted on its shoulder, he yanked his sword free of the skull. Before he even knew what he was doing, he hacked into the bear again. And again. He chopped the skull into bloody bits, screaming with wordless rage.

Finally, he fell to his knees in exhaustion.

Cold sweat had soaked through his tunic and breaches. It stung his eyes. He mopped his face with his palm, and his hand came away smeared in blood and brains. His chest was tight, heaving. The bear now blocked the doorway to the main hall. Where his torch was.

The mist had not crept in through the back door, but he wasn't about to take chances. He dug another torch from his travel bag and immediately set about trying to light it. With his trembling, bloody hands, it took a good many tries before it caught. When it did, he rose and drifted about the forge.

It was still in good condition, though he had naught to burn here, either. All the tools, though, they remained. In fact, these looked to have been forged from dverg steel as well. Maybe that was why they had remained rust-free after so many years. Nidavellir had traded with the Old Kingdoms. *Trade* was how the dvergar put it. In reality, they graced humanity with pittances, in exchange for slaves and sacrifices. Much as they did now, save the powerful Old Kingdoms might have received slightly better terms than the dying petty kingdoms now scattered across the North Realms.

A few more generations, perhaps, and if Mankind had not yet wiped itself out, the dvergar were like to enslave what remained. The age of man was ending fast. All the more reason for Volund and his brothers to remove themselves from these lands. He needed to find Altvir with all possible haste.

And yet … this place …

Volund ran his fingers over the masterful tools. With these, he could make almost aught. Things for trade, for information. The only reason he had to stay at this forge.

Spread the wealth around and someone must have seen Altvir.

The thought of her sparked fresh visions, and he slumped down to rest. Volund tossed the torch into the forge's fire pit and shut his eyes. He could almost see her. Feel her soft hands massaging his temples and banishing the need for fear or anger. Suppressing the rage and replacing it with light.

He needed her light.

4

AGILAZ

*T*he fortress of Halfhaugr was clearly named for the hill it sat on, a lopsided slope that looked to have been chopped off with an axe. A high wooden wall surrounded the town, in addition to the fortress proper, funneling travelers to a single gate nigh to the river. The town looked much like any well-defended settlement in Kvenland, in fact. Given the spearmen watching the gate, they expected trouble sooner or later.

No surprise. A day back, Agilaz and Hermod had passed through a battlefield lit with numerous pyres. The victors had burned the dead to keep them from rising, but had left skulls impaled on spears. Some of those skulls were small enough to have come from children. Agilaz could not stomach that, especially not with the way Hermod had looked at them. The local tribes warred with one another, as they so oft did. The Skalduns had slaughtered whole families in half the outlying lands between here and the sea. He and Hermod had sneaked past a war party leading away slaves not far from the battlefield.

The Halfhaugr men watched Agilaz and Hermod warily,

but made no move to bar their passage. A single man and a boy probably posed no threat in their minds. It gave them free rein in the town.

In any case, the fortress itself seemed the most obvious destination. The jarl would almost certainly have to put up a foreign guest, and his court might hold the information Agilaz sought.

The town itself consisted of perhaps two dozen houses, most of which had their own snow-crusted walls. The builders had clearly feared raiders, who would no doubt find Halfhaugr difficult pickings. On the other hand, perhaps that very defensibility had led the Skalduns to claim so many of the Hasding lands. If the Hasdingi retreated to this haven, they were, perhaps, less prepared to stand and fight over every last river, farm, or bog they might otherwise have claimed. One by one, they were losing their lands, and their fortress was becoming their prison.

A strong one, too.

"What're those marks on the walls?" Hermod asked, perhaps following his father's gaze.

"Dverg runes." Unlike his brother, Agilaz could not read them, but most likely they were intended to ward against the mist and its denizens. At least, he'd never known runes to protect against aught native to Midgard, man or beast.

"Did Uncle Volund make them?"

"Not these."

Twin doors stood open at the fortress threshold, protected by a scar-faced man leaning against one wall. He stood talking to a shieldmaiden in what appeared to be a very unsuccessful attempt to impress her.

Agilaz cleared his throat, and the man turned on him. "What do you want?"

"Information."

The man shrugged. "And who is asking?"

"I am Agilaz, a traveler from across the sea. I bring a silver handled knife, from Kvenland. A gift for your jarl." It was a treasure, granted him by his father. But material treasures meant very little without Olrun. He drew the blade, allowing the man to inspect the silver hilt.

After a quick look, the man jerked his head toward the inside, and Agilaz led Hermod in. Stone pillars supported a high roof. The doors led right into the great hall, the place lit by a large brazier, in addition to a fire pit, the whole place thick with smoke and the smell of mead.

Evening approached, and already the jarl and his men sat at a great table, drinking before the night meal. A few men boasted with each other about their hunts. Many, however, complained about food stores for the winter, or how much the Skaldun raids had cost them.

The jarl sat at the table's head. He looked up as Agilaz drew nigh.

"Boy," Agilaz said. "Take the jarl his gift."

Hermod did, running the dagger over and putting it on the table before the jarl.

The man's eyes sparkled with undisguised greed at the treasure. His wife, too, leaned close to inspect it. A young girl sat in her lap and reached for the blade until her father swatted her hand. "Very impressive. I am Jarl Hadding. Come, sit at my table."

Agilaz did so, and accepted the mead a slave brought. He drained it. Watered down. Even the stores of honey must be running low. "Your tribe faces war."

"What do you care?"

"I am looking for a particular warrior."

The jarl bit deep into a hunk of roasted meat. Venison, it looked like, though certainly not enough to go around. Still, you could not blame the jarl for eating and feeding his own family first. His closest thegns seemed fed, as well. Other warriors, less so, and some of the serving slaves looked gaunt as the dead. "Warrior have a name?" Hadding asked, juice dribbling into his blond beard.

"Olrun."

The men chuckled. "A shieldmaiden mercenary?" a red-haired one asked. "Your wife run off to join a war without you?"

Agilaz scowled at him. It was closer to the truth than the warrior probably realized, and Agilaz had no mood for such mockery, in jest or in earnest.

"Mmmm." The jarl spit out a bit of grease. "And you? Are you a mercenary?"

Getting caught up in the war did not seem wise, but then it might be his best chance to find Olrun. As a valkyrie, she could choose to hide herself from mortal eyes. But he had to believe that, if she saw him, she would come to him. She had to. Her ring had guided him here. His son would not grow up without a mother. Volund had done so, and it had haunted Agilaz's younger brother. Hermod would not suffer that urd.

"I might offer my services."

"For what?"

"A position in your court. A share of the plunder. Food." Those were what they'd expect him to ask for.

"Mmmm. You carry a bow. You good with it?"

"I am."

"Give us a show, then." The jarl pointed to a shield hanging on the far side of the hall. "Right in the middle, wanderer."

Agilaz rose slowly and unshouldered his weapon, sighing. A show. Boasting was a fool's game, but was sometimes something to be done for getting men's attention. He nocked an arrow. Hitting a shield dead center from across a room did not exactly pose a challenge.

He spun, releasing his shot. It slammed into the mug of the red-headed man who'd mocked him, shattering it right out of his hand. Watery mead exploded over the warrior, while the arrow continued onward to thunk into a different shield.

"Forgive me. I missed the target. Shall I shoot again?"

The warrior he'd drenched rose, sputtering, while the rest of the table burst into laughter.

"Sit down, Borje," Jarl Hadding commanded. "Brought that on yourself." He turned back to Agilaz. "What is it you think you can do for me?"

Agilaz sighed, then looked about the room. These thegns looked like they could fight, but they had not done so. His initial judgment had been right, he supposed. The Hasdingi had become trapped in the very haven they kept to protect themselves. "From the looks of it, you have fine enough warriors. But there is something I do well. I can sneak into your foe's camps, lead a small force. Harry them, destroy their supplies."

Borje wiped his face with a cloth a woman had given him. "The winter storms are coming."

"Which is why they will not expect it. I am an expert woodsman, and I know when a storm will break. I can find shelter for us and get us in and out of their—of *your*—stolen lands before they know we're there. By the time summer returns, they will be desperate to leave this place far behind. Let them turn their eyes to Hunaland or some other tribe and leave the Hasdingi be."

For that matter, if he killed enough men in battle, maybe a valkyrie would come for one of their souls.

"You are bold," Hadding said.

"In its own way, boldness can be wisdom."

"He's a fool," Borje said. "And he'll get anyone who follows him buried in the snow."

Agilaz favored the man with a withering gaze.

"You can't talk to my papa like that!" Hermod shouted.

A few men chuckled.

"I will need someone to provide for my son while I take such expeditions."

Hadding licked his fingers clean of grease. "The boy can stay here, in my hall. My wife and her ladies are already raising our daughter."

Good. Fostering his son with a jarl, even for a short time, might be good for the boy. A lesson learned firsthand was worth ten lectures. Hermod needed to understand the World, and the best way to do that was with new experiences.

"Who will come with me?" Agilaz asked.

After a few grumbles, a handful of men stood. Thegns and other free men, most likely, eager for plunder. Or starving, eager to steal food. Without the lost stores, the Hasdingi faced a hard winter and were like to lose a great many of their people.

A slave brought him a pathetic sliver of venison. Agilaz tore the greater portion of it off and handed it to Hermod, saving only enough to maintain his strength. "We leave at dawn, then. Before that, someone show me the lay of the land. I need to know what places you have lost."

ONE OF HADDING'S THEGNS, a man named Erik, took Agilaz to meet his wife, Liv. She had a map of the lands and began to point out the numerous hunting forts and few farms the Hasdingi had lost. North of them lay the Gandvik Sea. Agilaz had bartered passage there not so long ago, on one of the last ships to make the crossing before the next summer. They had landed at the Athra tribe's town, a whaling people. It was from the Athra he had learned of the Hasdingi's plight, a difficulty they had no interest in involving themselves in. So he had travelled south. Wherever men died valiant deaths, valkyries must follow.

Liv rolled up the map.

"Did you draw that yourself?" Agilaz asked.

"I did."

"Impressive."

The woman beamed at him.

Agilaz turned back to the thegn.

"They raided us all throughout the summer moons," Erik said. "We didn't realize it was so well planned until late."

Agilaz raised an eyebrow at that, and the thegn shrugged.

"There are always summer raids. A man defends his farm, a thegn holds each hunting fort. Men die. They took mine from me while I was out. Jarl Hadding couldn't spare the men to reclaim it." Erik spat.

That was what Agilaz was counting on. The more who died—good deaths, of course—the more likely he was to find Olrun. He needed his wife, and Hermod needed his mother. And if he had to kill some Skaldun raiders to make that happen, he'd do so. In truth, he would kill them all to get her back.

5

VOLUND

*A*ltvir's ring was a masterwork, a piece of beauty not quite like any of the jewels made in Nidavellir. Depending on how you looked at it, it might have been a dragon or a swan. And it had been wrought from orichalcum, the most precious of all metals. Orichalcum—the rosy gold—was found rarely in Midgard, and the dvergar treasured it above all other ores, above all treasures even. For it was stronger than even adamant and, more importantly, apt to soak up Megin. Or, souls, really. Enchanted items were forged from souls of unfortunate victims, hammered into metal. The greatest crafts of history, including all the famed runeblades of old, were made from souls bound to orichalcum. Dvalin and his kin had crafted the runeblades long ago, weapons without equal. Any weapon of ancient Art must be forged from orichalcum, but little of the ore remained.

The valkyries had rings of orichalcum, symbols that bound them in service to some eldritch power. And bound them to their husbands. If Volund could but understand the power of the rings, he might use it to immediately find

Altvir, maybe even to summon her back to him. Or even—he dared barely dream it—break the bond that tied her to that master of whom she feared to speak. Perhaps the rings held a piece of the valkyrie's soul, but he could not be certain.

And so, to understand it, he had forged seven duplicates at the forge in the ruined stone hall. Not of orichalcum, of course. The forge was stocked with iron and silver and even gold, but only those metals. With a fine chisel, he carved away, working every pattern the same. It didn't matter. He could make seven or seven hundred. The mysteries of the valkyrie's ring were not unraveling.

Still, he worked, the seventh ring almost finished. A little tap here. A little shaving there. It had to be perfect. If he was going to craft something, he would craft it without flaw. A master smith created naught less than a masterpiece. The dvergar had instilled that in him.

He feared they had instilled other things in him, too. His time in Nidavellir was when the darkness in his heart had first wakened, deep inside him. When the shadows had begun to move, to whisper to him as though they knew him well. They lied, claiming he belonged to them and need only welcome them. Perhaps—had he not met Altvir—he might have eventually heeded their call.

Volund blew metal shavings off the latest of his rings. It was flawless. Gold and silver entwined, married in elegance and beauty. It might bind a man and wife, but it had no secret power. He might have tried to infuse it with dvergar Art and bind a soul, but somehow he didn't think Altvir's ring came from them. No, the style of her ring was different, if somehow still familiar.

The duplicates would serve, however. In his days hunting, he had found a town not far, a trade center. People

passed through oft enough, and they would direct him. One
of these rings should buy him a lead on Altvir's location. It
must.

THE TOWN LAY on an icy crag above the fjord, making it
unapproachable on two sides. A thick wall encircled the rest
of it, no doubt intended to protect from the other six kingdoms as much as from trolls and dangers of the wild. It was
damned large, too. Several dozen houses gathered together
in mutual defense, all probably beholden to some king or
other. In the far distance, a castle rose up out of the moun-
tainside. No one built like that anymore. More remnants of
the Old Kingdoms, probably, but it was too far off to judge.

The gate guards had welcomed him in at the mention of
trade, and now he climbed the rocky path toward the town
center. There would be a market up there. Atop the path, a
wooden bridge spanned a small waterfall pitching down
into the fjord. Clumsy work that would not last a decade. Yet
one more example of modern man's vain attempt to assert
the slightest dominance over nature. The bridge creaked
under his boots as he strolled toward the market. Volund
shook his head. He could have built a better bridge in his
sleep. Did the artisan take no pride in his craft? None at all?

In the square, he paused before a cobbler's shop. His
boots were worn almost through, and that was one thing he
could not so easily make. After inspecting the lot of them—
all serviceable, in a handful of different sizes—he broke off a
piece of his arm ring. A tiny shard of silver, but more than
enough for a good pair of boots. The cobbler grunted at him
and tossed him a pair.

Volund frowned. How could the man know which size

he needed? He slouched down on a rock and yanked his old boots off. His toes had turned slightly yellow, and he had to massage warmth back into them before he tried on the new boots. They sat snugly, as close a fit as he'd ever had. Cobbler knew his trade after all.

And everyone needed shoes. Especially men going off to battle, marching long distances.

"Who rules here?" Volund asked.

"King Nidud." The man arched his neck toward the castle in the distance, then spit for emphasis.

Volund refrained from comment. Dvergar were known to do the same. Most Men were, in fact, vulgar, it seemed. And to a prince of Kvenland, it seemed quite vulgar. "Not a just king, then?"

The man spit again, the only answer forthcoming.

So not just—but then, who was? Power settled upon the corrupt, the one drawn to the other in an endless cycle. Such was the way of the World. And if this Nidud was not generous with his people, perhaps he was at least ambitious. "Men come through here. Do they speak of wars?"

The cobbler grunted, then looked to the sword hanging over Volund's shoulder. "You a mercenary?"

Volund might have told him he was searching for a valkyrie. The man might have laughed or might have told him best to die in battle then. Either way, it did not seem like to get him anywhere. Instead, he drew one of the silver rings from his pouch. "I am a smith. Where there is war, one finds profit." The cobbler would understand profit.

The man's eyes flashed hungrily at the ring. Perhaps enough wealth to change his life. At the least, it would ensure he lived well through the next winter. But such treasures meant naught without Altvir. They were pittances compared to the jewel of his wife. The thought of it left his stomach roiling and shadows playing upon his periphery. Without warning, an urge built in his gut, the need to seize the cobbler and beat the answers from him. Volund bit his tongue, trying to still the sick feeling. The man had done naught to warrant such violence.

"The king raised a levy last moon, took a great number of men. Some say they raided east, but talk is more that they went to challenge one of those barbarian tribes in the south."

"The Aesir?"

The cobbler spat in apparent agreement. He would spit less if Volund smashed his jaw. Drool through broken teeth, perhaps.

Volund forced his hands to his side. "Which tribe?"

"How the fuck would I know that?" A shattered nose would improve his face.

Volund shook his head slowly and dropped the ring in the snow before the man's shop. Let the useless, vulgar man dig it out.

He turned away. It was a start, in any event. If a Sviarland king raided or warred with an Ás tribe, surely glorious battles would ensue. Battles and honorable deaths. Those deaths would draw valkyries, maybe many of them. And if Nidud had spread his schemes over several locations, it might explain why the three valkyries had flown in different directions. But what did this little king hope to gain by provoking the Aesir? To the Sviarlanders, they were naught but barbarians, feared for their mystique, their savagery, and the berserkir and varulfur often found within the tribes.

If the king could claim their land, he might grow rich. But more likely, he would find himself raided by one tribe after another. The Ás tribes shared no love between them, but Volund doubted they wanted their land taken by foreigners. Of course, those barbarians themselves had swept in and stolen that same land some few generations back. They claimed Aujum as their own, enslaving most of the natives—those who were not killed or driven out as refugees.

The truth was, it didn't much matter to Volund if the Sviarlanders and the Aesir all killed one another. In fact, it might make it easier to find Altvir.

Volund made his way back toward the bridge. He would return to the ruin. If he hurried, he could make it before dark. Then at sunrise he could head south, try to find the battlefields. He ought not to travel at night. Yet somehow, he wasn't certain why it should frighten him. With a torch, a man could move at night. But all wisdom urged one not to. The vaettir were most active then.

No, he would go with first light.

THE FORGE'S fire held blessed warmth. Volund slumped down with his back against it, letting the heat seep into his chilled flesh. He always slept in here these days. He'd cut the bear's hide and made a fine bed from it. Besides, the forge comforted him. The smell of thick smoke lingered long after he'd last worked iron, and the tools themselves seemed wont to sing him to sleep.

Sleep came easy. Easy, but rarely restful. In his dreams, he saw the deep places of Nidavellir, dancing in his memories like the play of shadows cast from torchlight in halls beneath the mountains. A domain of rock and iron and gemstones, glimpsed ever in half-light. The dvergar themselves could see as well in shadows as any cat, and after two years in such a habitat, even Volund had become accustomed to it. So much so that, back then, the sun used to sting his eyes on the rare occasions he saw it.

That expanse called him back, welcomed him into the darkness and whispered to him secrets no mortal could know. For there were Otherworlds beyond Midgard, worlds from which the vaettir came. And those worlds knew more, knew deeper truths. The dvergar were like that too, alien to this world, privy to lore that might make a völva piss herself in horror. They had bored up through the ground and, having no form in this world, taken mortal hosts. Twisted their shapes to their liking, into gnarled, swarthy old men and women. Their spines would bend and twist and shrink until a dverg stood no taller than a man's shoulder.

And before even the Old Kingdoms, they had begun to build, to craft, and to dominate the deep places. They took slaves as workers, messengers, and sometimes, as hosts for more dverg souls. Volund supposed he was lucky that had not been his urd.

6

DAYS GONE

Eleven Years Ago

*A*t twelve winters, Volund was at last a man, and his father was taking him to learn a trade. So Slagfid had teased him, that he—a prince of Kvenland—should be apprenticed to a smith instead of fostered with a great noble. Those teasings were hollow, though, and Volund had to smile. After all, he would serve under no mortal smith at all, but in the court of Nidavellir.

The mountainous land of the dvergar—dwarves, as Men sometimes called them—lay far to the west of his homeland. Father had taken a dogsled, intent on escorting him personally. And for days they had raced forward, trailed behind by guards Volund's grandfather, the king, had sent to watch over his bastard son and grandsons. Only Volund's brother Slagfid was with them, for Agilaz had remained behind to continue his own apprenticeship as a woodsman.

Volund was glad to have one of his brothers along, though he might have preferred Agilaz's quiet support to Slagfid's ribbing.

The woods of Kvenland had given way to the hills and then the great mountains of Nidavellir.

Never had Volund seen or imagined such towering behemoths. The peaks stretched up, above the mists, scraping the sky. Though beautiful, the frozen range had also slowed their progress, as Father navigated narrow passes on the sleds. And this morning, they'd been forced to leave even the dogs behind, in the care of the hound-master, until his father would return.

Without Volund.

He had not understood the finality of that, not in truth. Not until they'd come upon the slave camp here and Father had asked for those final directions. As Father and the guards traded for provisions, Volund watched from the edge of the small camp. A stone fence ringed three stone build-ings, each so covered in ice and snow one could easily miss them.

Volund's heart pounded against his ribcage. Gods, he felt he had to piss three times an hour. And here, in these icy passes, fumbling with his trousers was a painful, drawn-out process. Slagfid chuckled at his nervousness—perhaps to cover his own. Atop this slope they were supposed to find the entrance, if the slaves were to be believed.

No matter how good-natured his brother intended the jests, Volund did not need them now. Not when he was about to meet his new master, a being not even a Man.

The dvergar did not like to come out into the open air, especially in daylight. Some legends claimed sunlight would turn them to stone, but Volund found that hard to credit. But then, who knew? Dvergar were somewhat Otherworldly, after all. They guarded their secrets closely. Around the campfires, sometimes the men called them immortal, called them spirits—the term was *vaettir* in this land. An old wizard had come to the court two winters back, a wanderer who fascinated and terrified in equal measure. He had spoken of the wonders wrought in the deep forges of Nidavellir, of treasures from the bowels of the land and of crafts unmatched.

No doubt that was when Father had first gotten the idea his son ought to become a smith. And no apprenticeship with any mere armorer would do for the son of a prince of Kvenland. No, Father had set his heart that his son would learn the secret arts of Nidavellir. And the king had indulged Father, sent emissaries. And to everyone's surprise, the dvergar had granted the request.

A slave girl approached Volund, bearing a skin. She was bundled tight in mammoth hide, several layers of it, including a hood that shaded her face.

"Water?" he asked.

"Ale. They give it to us to keep us warm out here."

Volund took the skin and had a long swig. It did warm him, pleasantly. After wiping his mouth, he returned the skin. "You've seen them?"

The girl nodded.

Shame he couldn't get a good look at her face. One could tell what someone really thought from their eyes. The girl said naught else though, just stood there.

Finally Volund glanced back at his father, who was still deep in conversation with the slaves. The slave girl still stared at him. "Was there something else?"

"I ... I'm to make you a man now."

Volund stood there, mouth hanging open. The dashing prince of Kvenland, not able to form a response to a dvergar slave. Why would she ... Who would send her for that? Gods, he needed to piss again. And he thought his heart was pounding before. "I, uh ..."

The girl took his hand and began leading him toward one of the buildings.

This was really happening. Frey's flaming sword, it was happening now. "I need ... um, give me a moment. I'll meet you inside."

She cocked her head strangely, but ducked into the snow-crusted house without further comment. Volund shuddered and glanced back at Slagfid. His brother offered him an encouraging wave. Well, he probably meant it to be encouraging. Gods, high and low!

Volund stepped around back and relieved himself. Then he took a deep breath. Then a few more.

When he entered the house, the girl had shed her furs and was lying on them, stripped down to her woolen chemise. Now he could see her face, and she was young. Maybe as young as he was.

"I've had my bleeds," she said, as if he had asked such a thing.

"Why are you doing this?" he asked instead.

The girl looked at him like he was an imbecile. "Because they tell us to. They want ... they said you should have your needs seen to before you arrive."

She pulled off her chemise, exposing tiny breasts. She had done this before, she must have. The dvergar must have ... It was so hard to think with her lying there, waiting for him.

Volund knelt beside her, reached for her. His hand was shaking. His hand didn't shake when he held a sword or bow or aught else. His hands never shook. The girl pulled his hand slowly down onto her chest, and then his face to hers. He had kissed a girl once or twice.

But not like this.

LATER, after they had left the slave camp far behind, he had realized: he had never even asked her name. She had suffered his awkward fumbling, his confusion. He'd wanted to ask Father about her, but the sly stares and chuckles of the other men had stilled his tongue.

And Slagfid's questions he ignored as best he was able. His brother had known a girl or three, or claimed so.

"You did not embarrass yourself too much, I hope?"

Volund grunted. Agilaz would not have asked and would not have expected an answer had he done so. Slagfid was Mist-mad if he expected one.

So he climbed so deep into his own thoughts that finding himself approaching the gates of Nidavellir had caught him unaware. A plateau opened up above the path, as though a primeval frost jotunn had scooped out a chunk of the peak and tossed it aside. Worked stone covered that plateau, including twin towers, upon which human archers watched their approach. Beyond those towers, at the back of the ice-coated platform, rose double doors five times the height of a man, each carved with elegant designs and intricate runes.

Atop the path, their whole group paused, staring. Some few of the guards had made this trek before, and thus knew the way. They had come with the offer of apprenticeship in the first place and, before that, had even made the tribute. Once every decade, Kvenland sent a tribute of gold, silver, food, slaves. Aught they could spare. Yes, Nidavellir was far. But none wanted to arouse the ire of the dvergar by seeming to slight them in their due.

The dvergar were still vaettir, beings from a Realm

beyond Midgard. That they deigned to have peaceful dealings with Mankind was a blessing.

Father waved back at the pair of guards carrying a heavy
chest. He had bought an apprenticeship for his son by
offering Volund's weight in gold. The men trudged forward,
hiding any weariness they felt. Perhaps fear had buried it.
They deposited the chest before the great gates and then
scrambled backward.

Father cleared his throat. "I am Wade, Prince of Kvenland. As promised, I deliver this gold to you."

No answer was forthcoming. Volund glanced around.
The men had begun to do the same, murmuring to themselves, or staring up at the archers in the towers. Great
braziers lit the tops of the towers, making it hard to see the
men standing before them. Eventually, one pointed at the
sun which had just begun to dip below the horizon.

The stories spoke truth, then. The dvergar would not
venture out in daylight. Draugar, trolls—so many beings
from beyond the Mortal Realm seemed to shun the light.
He'd heard a story, once, that sunlight even burned the svartalfar. The liosalfar walked in sunlight, but then they did not
come to Midgard often.

Volund folded his arms, watching the setting sun. Up
here, above the mist, it cast the World in brilliant shades.
But it was setting behind the mountains, and from this
side he could not revel in its true glory. Instead he looked
east. Back where his home lay. What madness had
possessed Father to make such a deal with Nidavellir? And
why had Volund so readily agreed, felt so honored? The
thought of becoming the greatest craftsman in the North
Realms had seemed too good to be true. He'd imagined
himself returning home in glory. Men would trek for days
and weeks to trade for the goods he made. Or so he'd

allowed himself to believe, half-drunk on a wandering wizard's tale.

Standing on a freezing mountain, waiting for beings who shunned the sunlight ... the prospect seemed different now. It seemed a fancy born of Mist-madness and hubris.

As the sun vanished behind the mountains, ice crunched and stone creaked. The great doors seemed to open of their own accord, drawn inward. The hall they revealed was dimly lit by sconces on the walls, spaced too far apart for Volund's liking. And yet, somehow, the deep shadows lurking behind the massive columns seemed to welcome him, to call him inward. And the longer he stared, the more his fear melted away. Why had he feared such a place of grandeur? No work of man could compare to these vaulted ceilings, these columns so wide no two men could stretch their arms around them.

A pair of hooded men emerged from the long hall. All stood silently, watching, as those men approached. Without a word they exited the gates, took up the chest, and began to plod back inside.

And should Volund follow them? "Father?"

"I don't ..."

It was all right. Volund knew what he had to do. They had come here for but one reason. He embraced his father.

Slagfid clapped him on the shoulder, seeming lost for words. For once.

Volund nodded at his brother. And then he walked into the shadows of Nidavellir.

His footsteps echoed on the stone floor as he trod after the chest-bearers.

They walked a long time, but with each step, Volund's heart grew a little lighter. His eyes were quickly adapting to the darkness. Still, when the sound of the closing doors rang through the hall, he could not help but cringe. They shut with a resounding clang that heralded a true finality one could not deny, like the revelation of urd.

Volund blew out a breath and hurried after the chest-bearers.

Those men paused before a stocky figure not even Volund's height. The man had a thick beard, a bulbous nose, and a swarthy face covered in pock-marks. He waved his hand, and the bearers dropped the chest and then opened it, revealing the golden offerings. Goblets, coins, and jewelry lay in a pile in the chest. Volund shifted from foot to foot as the dverg bent to examine the offerings.

The creature picked up a few pieces and tasted them, before tossing them back in the chest. With another motion of his hand he directed the human servants to carry it on down the hall. They did so, and the dverg next waddled over to Volund, looking him up and down.

With a rough, calloused hand, he grabbed Volund's chin and squeezed his jaw. The pressure opened his mouth, and the dverg looked inside, seeming to inspect his teeth. Volund tried to pull away, but the dverg's grip was like an iron vise. When the creature released him, he fell backward, landing on his arse. There was pretty much no way to make that look dignified, so he rose slowly, trying to make no show of the pain it had caused him.

"You are suited to it." His voice was deep, rumbly like an avalanche. "I am Dvalin, son of King Modsognir. You will call me Master. Address any of my kind without proper respect and an iron spike shall be pounded through your tongue. Am I understood?"

No one had ever addressed him like that, but objecting seemed the epitome of foolhardiness, so Volund bowed. "Yes, Master. I am Volund, son of Wade, son of ..."

Dvalin held up a hand. "Mortal lineages are as interesting to me as the lineages of rats are to you. Follow me." The dverg began to shamble down the hall, leaving Volund to chase after him. Because his master took such short, awkward strides, Volund had to pause repeatedly to let Dvalin stay ahead of him. "Like any lump of ore, you will be useless until heated, tested, and tempered. First, we shall have you beaten to see how much you can take and remain conscious."

"But—"

"Silence. When you are to speak, I will tell you."

Volund snapped his mouth shut. Had his father known what the apprenticeship would entail? Unlikely. No man had ever received such an ... honor.

"After the beatings, you will be burned. Later lashed, raped, and drowned. If none of that breaks you, then, student, your real training begins."

Volund faltered, staring back down the long hall. The doors were shut. It was far too late to run.

7

AGILAZ

They returned from the last raid mere hours before the storm hit. Agilaz had known the storm was coming and pushed his little party hard to reach Halfhaugr. Nineteen men had set out with him this time, and seventeen would return. All in all, two deaths on their side had bought nigh a dozen Skaldun corpses. More importantly, they returned laden with bags of turnips, kale, chard. It would help see Halfhaugr through the winter. Spirits were high among the men as the gates were thrown wide.

"Four raids and four victories," Erik said. "Frey's sword, man. You move like a ghost."

Agilaz clapped him on the shoulder. "You don't have to be any such thing. Think to move as a wolf moves, at home in the woods. Unafraid of shadows."

Erik volunteered for every raid, and, in the past two, had begun to ask about Agilaz's tactics. Agilaz had told him hunting men was like hunting game, save men did not smell you coming. Kill a man who did not see you, and you lived longer. It was a lesson he had learned early. Yes, some warriors disdained it, they relished a fair fight. Such men tended to live shorter lives.

Erik snorted. "Shadows hold plenty worth fearing, in my experience. Ask any völva, she'll tell you."

Agilaz nodded. Erik had a point, he supposed.

Leaving the others behind, Agilaz hurried back to the jarl's hall. Hermod greeted him as soon as he entered, followed by the jarl's daughter, Frigg. She was always chasing after Hermod these days. The girl claimed she'd grow up to be a shieldmaiden. She did not yet understand her parents would never allow her such a path. A jarl's daughter was too valuable a political tool.

Agilaz swept his son up in his arms and held him close.

"Did you find mama?"

"No. Not yet."

"A shame," Liv said. Erik's wife stood nearby, offering him a wan smile. She had coaxed enough of his tale out of him to know what he sought. Olrun's true nature he did not reveal. No one would have believed him, even had he the inclination to share.

Before he could answer, Erik grabbed his wife and carried her off, laughing and sputtering.

Agilaz roughed Hermod's hair. "Go on. Play with Frigg."

"She's a girl."

"You may not always think that a bad thing. Be generous and courteous until someone gives you a reason not to, boy."

Hermod sighed as though being put upon and rolled his eyes at the girl. This would be her second winter, and already Agilaz had no doubt she would grow up pretty. Wise too, he hoped. Until Hadding's wife, Fjorgyn, gave him a son, Frigg was his sole heir, and the man must already be pushing thirty winters. He did not have long left to sire sons.

Moreover, his brother Alci was the jarl of the Godwulfs, and, as a varulf, would live long enough to become a threat to the Hasdingi, should Hadding have no male heir.

Agilaz and Olrun had oft spoken of having another child, a sister maybe, for Hermod. The valkyrie spoke of how she would raise a girl, of the things she would teach her. Agilaz could almost see such a child in Frigg.

Agilaz had not made it far before the jarl received him with open arms. "By Frey, man, they tell me you come back victorious again. How do you do it?"

Agilaz shrugged. "Most oft, by killing men not ready for battle."

Hadding rocked back on his heels, then shook his head. "Be that as it may ..." He patted the broadsword slung over his shoulder. "Next time I will go with you myself. When will the storm break?"

They always misunderstood him. Agilaz could spot signs of the changing weather, patterns of behavior in the animals, the feel of the air. He was not some völva with knowledge of the future, and he didn't know when a storm was going to end, only when it drew nigh. "We should feast tonight, my jarl. The days have grown short enough already, and I am weary."

Hadding laughed. "Fine. Keep your mysteries, hunter. You're fast becoming a legend around here, after all. And what good is a legend without his secrets?"

Agilaz could only shake his head. All he wanted was to find his wife. The days were short, and the nights without her very long indeed. Olrun had a quietness to her, a peaceful air that drew all to stillness and let him sleep in comfort. Sometimes she would sing to him, sing to Hermod. If he held the ring close enough, he could still hear that song. He rubbed the ring with his thumb. Its warmth was all he had—that and Hermod.

But she was nigh, he could feel her. Every moment seemed to bring her closer. When winter abated, the Hasdingi would face war. Pitched battles must surely summon Olrun, but he did not want to wait moons more to see his wife. He did not want to wait a single night longer.

So he took no real pleasure in the drunken feasts and laughter that went on, long into the night. He did not find laughter in Erik or Liv's jokes, nor did he care for the praise and glory Hadding heaped on him. He did, however, note that Borje still looked upon him with disdain. The warrior, too proud now to join the raids under Agilaz's command, had grown ever more bitter. He had the look of a wolf wanting to take down a bear.

Agilaz would have to keep up his guard, draw his allies closer. A wolf would not strike alone, but even a bear was no match for an entire wolf pack.

IN THE NIGHT, he tossed and turned. He slept in a fur-lined alcove, in the room Hadding had provided to him. It was nice enough and held its own little brazier to keep the chill away. Still, he rarely slept well without her. If he closed his eyes and concentrated on the ring, he could feel her presence. That was all that ever let him rest.

The door creaked open. Agilaz's eyes latched onto the figure slipping into the room, a man by his silhouette. Followed by another. Agilaz closed his fingers around a knife under his furs. Two men, and he could catch only one by surprise, if that.

It took all he had to resist the urge to leap up. Hermod

slept in another alcove on the far side of the brazier. He couldn't see his son without rising. And one of the men had drifted in that direction, one toward him. But move too soon and he would lose his only advantage. The right moment was what counted.

As one man drew nigh, the glint of firelight reflected off a blade. Agilaz surged upward, flinging himself at the stalker. His weight bore them both crashing into the brazier, his victim screaming. Agilaz planted the knife in the figure's throat. Blood exploded into his eyes, half blinding him.

Hermod screamed.

Agilaz rolled away from the flames and rose in a fighting crouch, while rubbing his other arm over his face to clear his eyes. The other figure slammed into him as he did so, shoving them both backward.

"Hermod, run!" Agilaz shouted.

The fallen man had caught fire. Flames leapt from his body to the furs around the room.

His attacker pushed a knife forward, closer and closer to Agilaz's face, despite Agilaz's strain to hold him back. As the man leaned in, he knew him.

"Erik?"

He wanted to ask why, but his erstwhile friend only struggled all the harder, roaring as he tried to drive the blade downward. Agilaz twisted to the side, and the blade scraped off the wall. He shoved Erik, and the man fell over backward, pitching into the spreading flames.

Agilaz scrambled to the side, panting, coughing on the rapidly expanding smoke. He couldn't breathe, couldn't see. He fell to his knees.

"Hermod!" his voice came out as a hacking rasp. Frey, please say the boy had fled the room.

Half walking, half crawling, he stumbled forward. Heat

washed over his face, singed his bare arms as he scrambled toward the doorway.

He had only just reached it when someone yanked him upward. Agilaz blinked, coughed. Tried to see.

Jarl Hadding held him up.

"H-Hermod ..." Agilaz gasped.

His son screamed from inside the room.

Agilaz's stomach lurched. No. No!

He jerked free of Hadding's grasp and stumbled back into the room. Flames engulfed it. Smoke so thick he couldn't see a fucking thing. "Hermod!"

Even shouting drew in a lungful of smoke.

"Papa!"

Agilaz crawled forward, trying to stay under the smoke cloud. Ash stung his eyes. His boy was kneeling over Erik's smoldering corpse. Borje's knife stuck in the man's chest.

Fuck.

Agilaz lunged forward, grabbed his son, and yanked him through the flames. Hermod screamed. No other way. He shoved the boy out toward the door.

Hacking, coughing, he tried to crawl. His legs weren't moving right.

"Papa!" From outside. Hermod had escaped, praise Frey.

Rough hands seized him even as his vision faded.

AGILAZ WOKE IN A SMALL CHAMBER. Barred and guarded. The man had ordered him to wait. Wait while Hadding deliberated. Agilaz had pounded on the door when the man had refused to speak of Hermod. The ash wood did not budge.

Finally, he had collapsed back to the floor. Breathing hurt.

Earlier that same evening, Agilaz had told Erik the key to victory was to attack like a wolf. Move silently through the shadows. Now, the man had tried to kill him in his sleep and paid for it with his life. As well he should. If aught had happened to Hermod ... Hel take both those traitorous troll-fuckers.

The burns on his arm stung, a constant pain and reminder of his brush with death. Where was Hermod?

They were lucky this place was built from stone. It must have contained the blaze. Must have been old work, strong. Volund knew about that kind of thing. Damn, but he hoped his brothers had had better luck finding their wives than he had his. They ought to all have passed the winter at Wolf Lake, huddled around a fire, roasting snow hares and telling stories of far-off places. Instead, he was a prisoner, his brothers gone to unknown lands.

The door creaked open, and Hadding stepped in. He did not bring in his guards, and he shut the door behind him. Good signs.

"Where is my son?"

"His arm was burned. My völva is treating him."

He lived. The mountain crushing Agilaz's gut lightened. "The wound is bad?"

"He might have a scar. Brave boy. Five winters behind him, and he's killed a thegn." Hadding folded his arms.

Agilaz lurched to his feet, trying to ignore the pain. "To defend his father from a murderer!"

"Peace, Agilaz. I know *why* Hermod acted such. Still, I find myself in a difficult situation. My thegn's actions were criminal, at least on the surface. But Erik's friends claim you fancied his wife."

"Liv?" That was absurd. He had spoken to her, and she

was oft friendly, but naught more. "I am a married man. I'd sooner cut off my own hand than betray my wife."

Hadding frowned. "Very good. Then why do they think this?"

Agilaz rose and shook his head. Now he was to answer why aught went on in another man's head? He spread his hands. "Borje has never liked my position here. Maybe he planted the idea in Erik's head. We were all drunk last night."

"Yes, I remember. I was not so drunk to not see Liv leaning on your shoulder on more than one occasion."

That ... had happened. "It was not like that."

"You want her?"

"No!"

Hadding nodded and scratched his beard. "I'm not going to lie. It looks bad, Agilaz. If you were to lie with the woman, people would talk."

"I have no intention of lying with her or any other woman, save my wife."

"Good. I will keep her here, at Halfhaugr." The jarl waved a hand at him. "And you will take Vestborg back for me. If you retake it, I will grant it to you."

Erik's home. They had not struck there because it was too far out. It was on the natural boundary between the Hasding lands and those of the Skalduns. Had Erik not lost the fort early in the summer, things might have gone differently.

Agilaz rubbed his brow. "That sounds like a job for an army, not a small party of raiders."

"Not if you get in there and kill the thegn who holds it. With him gone, the others would retreat, and we could take the fort. Do that, and I'll grant you Erik's position, land, and title."

Damn. Agilaz did not so much care about being a thegn, but he could not afford to lose Hadding as an ally. He still needed to be on one side or the other of this impending war if he was to find Olrun. And the chance to own a whole hunting fort, so much land ... it did have a certain appeal.

"So be it. I shall kill your enemy for you, jarl."

8

VOLUND

Fits held Volund, tried to throttle him with memories. Part of him longed to go back there, back to Nidavellir. Why should he wish such a thing? His apprenticeship had cost him all he had. But it had made him all he was. A craftsman without peer among Mankind. Even, sometimes, he thought the dvergar had begun to envy his talent. Maybe that was the origin of his true woes.

Cold iron clanked around his wrist, and he jerked awake. A half dozen men were in his forge. He lunged for the nearest, the one who had manacled his wrist as he slept. He caught the man's throat and squeezed. That pathetic, squirming life seeped out, eyes bulging, tongue lolling. Blows rained on the side of Volund's head, and he fell.

He tried to rise, but manacles bound his feet too. Someone kicked him in the face.

§

HOT WATER SPRAYED over his face. Volund coughed, rolled over. Gods, that smell. The man he'd choked stood, pissing on him, laughing, along with his men. Volund surged upward, but two of the other men grabbed his arms.

"Thought that might wake you," the first man said as he fastened his trousers.

Volund spit in his direction. Sometimes vulgarity was called for, even from a prince. Such was the way of the World.

"You assaulted a thegn of the king. I could have your head for that."

Volund sneered. "My king is back in Kvenland."

The men chuckled. "Now your king is Nidud, smith. And your king wishes to meet you."

"Believe me. He truly does not. Release me now, else you shall rue this day for the rest of your miserable life."

The thegn backhanded him. The blow left Volund dazed, only half-aware as the men dragged him from the forge.

As his vision cleared, he spied the man at the front. Wearing Volund's sword. The temerity of it set his blood roiling afresh, and strange shadows playing at his periphery.

He might charge forward, maybe even break the grip of these two if he caught them unaware. Perhaps he might strangle the thegn with his manacles. But he could not over-power five other men, especially not unarmed and chained.

And so he walked. The dvergar had taught him naught if not patience. One struck only when the iron was hot enough.

With the right timing, the right temperature, even the strongest of metals could be beaten into submission. And men were not nigh so strong.

IN TRUTH, he ought not to have shown the cobbler such wealth. Or perhaps he simply should not have insulted the man by dropping the ring. Or he ought to have just killed him. A dead man tells his king very little.

Volund's own ring seemed cold now, the heartbeat had grown faint. They were taking him the wrong way.

They marched him around the same town and up the long, broken path toward the castle. The closer they drew, the more certain he became. This Nidud did not occupy any fortress of the Old Kingdoms, but a place built by the dvergar themselves. A great platform extended out of a sheer cliff face, a vista from which the king must be able to see out over the mists. So high even birds seemed to fly only beneath that peak. And the mighty arch that delved into the mountain must lead to deep tunnels, mines, and all the workings of olden days.

The Old Kingdoms had, on very rare occasions, taken such places from the dvergar. Some of those kingdoms had patrons among the Vanir. Perhaps one of them had helped capture this place. And yet, such a fortress was nigh unassailable. The only approach from outside was a narrow, winding path along the mountain's edge. No more than one man at a time could pass that way. From the battlements, a single archer with half Agilaz's skill could hold back an army.

Most like then, this place had fallen to the Niflungar. Their sorcery—powers drawn and learned from the cursed goddess, Hel—that alone might have given them ingress to the fortress. But like all the Old Kingdoms, the Niflungar had collapsed into a shadow of their former glory, and they, too, had abandoned many of their outposts. Left them for petty kings like Nidud to hold and think himself great, think himself worthy of a legacy he could not begin to understand.

Volund found himself shaking his head as the king's men forced him up that path. "Men know the dvergar are famed for their metalcraft and stonework. But did you know they work with almost aught you can imagine?"

The lead thegn glanced back at him. "Shut your fucking mouth, smith."

"I've seen them make daggers of human bone you would swear is walrus ivory."

"I will throw you from this mountain if you do not shut your mouth."

"No. You won't. You did not bring me all this way to kill me. You brought me here to meet your king. Probably he wants me to craft something for him, some great work. And perhaps I shall. I just want you to know, I shall carve it from your bones. And your king will thank me for it, for it shall be the finest work he has ever seen."

The thegn spat at him. Volund smiled.

THE GREAT HALL rose at least fifty feet high, ending in a vaulted ceiling lost in dancing shadows. Did the others see that dance? Did the ever-encroaching darkness move before their eyes as it did before his? Volund suspected not. If they had seen what he saw, they would run from the place, screaming for völvur to ward them against the night.

At the back of this hall sat a king and queen. The man was ancient, his long hair gone gray, his beard threadbare. He must have reached twice the age a man ought. What more could this king want from his life? He was rotting and withering away and would have best met his end on a battlefield. Or perhaps that was his intent. Perhaps that was why he started this war, to meet a final, glorious end.

His queen was younger, though by no means young. Perhaps forty winters, and certainly nigh unto the end of her life, as well. Streaks of gray ran through her blonde hair, and she watched Volund's approach with wary eyes. Oh yes —she knew they had brought something dangerous into their midst. In their arrogance, they chained a cave bear and thought they could control it. But sooner or later, wild beasts always escaped their chains. Woe be upon those who dared try to master them.

"Well, Thakkrad. I see you return with your prize."

The thegn shoved Volund forward hard enough he fell to his knees a few feet from the king's throne. More like than not, Volund could leap up, strangle the king and the queen both. Of course, then Thakkrad really would throw him off the mountain. Instead, Volund raised his eyes to meet first the king's gaze, then the queen's.

Nidud licked his lips, while his queen averted her eyes.

"What is it you wish, king?" Volund asked.

Nidud rose slowly, a pop echoing from his spine, followed by his slight groan. The dverg architecture was designed with such perfect acoustics the sound carried throughout the entire great hall. Why did the men follow such an elderly king? Had he earned such loyalty in his younger days? More likely he'd bought it with treasures stolen from this ancient place.

"The townsfolk speak of a smith with talent worthy of song. Some say you seek employment in my wars." Nidud spread his hands. "And you have found it."

"You want me to forge a weapon for you?"

"A weapon? I want you to forge an armory. You will outfit every thegn under my command with such arms and such protection none can stand against them. Do this, and you shall have your weight in gold."

Volund rose slowly enough that Thakkrad made no move to stop him. His weight in gold? His father had once paid that price, though Volund was a man now, with thick muscles and much greater weight. "I have no time for such lengthy endeavors, king. Nor do I find your men's hospitality sufficient to warrant any such arrangement."

Nidud groaned, stretching his back before answering. "You seem to have misunderstood. You shall do this work."

"Or what? You'll kill me?" Volund smirked. "Then you will have naught to show for it." He jerked his head back toward Thakkrad. "Give me this one's head and I'll make a sword for you the likes of which you have never seen."

The king arched an eyebrow and glanced at Thakkrad. Volund kept his eyes forward, watching the queen, but the sound of the thegn squirming back there almost made him smile. "Thakkrad," the king said, "our guest needs encouragement. Hang him from the platform."

The thegn chuckled back there, and this time, Volund couldn't help but look at him. The man winked before seizing him by the shoulder.

Before he was taken anywhere, the queen rose and whispered something in the king's ear. Nidud's eyes went to Volund's hand, and he grunted.

"Hold his hand."

The thegn grabbed Volund's wrist. Volund slammed his elbow into the man's face. Cartilage shattered under the blow and the thegn fell, blood gushing between his fingers.

Several more men rushed forward and drove Volund back to his knees.

The king shook his head and rolled his eyes at the thegn.

"I'm half tempted to let the smith have your head after that foolery. Get his hand."

Blood streaming down his face, Thakkrad did as the king commanded and grabbed Volund's wrist with both of his own. Volund strained, but could not pry his arm free from the man's grasp. Slowly, the thegn pulled it forward.

"What in the fathomless dark of Svartalfheim do you think—"

Nidud grabbed his hand and yanked Altvir's ring from his little finger.

"No!" Not that. "Do not touch it!"

"My wife seems to think the princess will find this a prize." The king held the orichalcum band up before his eyes, examining it. "Such exquisite work. Yes, let Bodvild have this." He returned to his throne and handed the ring to the queen. Then he waved a hand. "Get on with it. The platform."

"No!" How dare he? Altvir's ring was for him alone, his gift, his blessing. His solace in the darkness. Without it, he could never find her. Never even find himself.

They dragged him away from the throne, even as he raged, pulled against their grasp. He could not lose that ring. It would never be allowed to grace the hand of another. Never. "I will bring ruination upon your entire line! Return it to me or the skalds will tell of your vile urd for a thousand years! You shall reap horrors for this, king!"

Six men hefted him into the air and carried him from the great hall, out onto the platform. The men flung him onto the freezing ground, the impact sending jolts of pain through his limbs. Thakkrad attached another chain to the manacles on his feet, this one running from a great iron ring embedded in the stone.

Two other men grabbed his arms and dragged him toward the edge.

"Return my ring!"

"Go fuck a troll. Assuming your cock doesn't freeze off." Thakkrad shoved him.

For a heartbeat he fell through the air, icy wind stripping his scream. Then the chain jerked him to a sudden stop, a feeling like his legs had been ripped out from their sockets. He'd fallen only a dozen feet, but now hung in open air, swinging back and forth beneath the platform.

Hanging upside down here, he had an excellent view of the masterful buttresses supporting the platform. His cloak fell away, denying him even the slightest ward against the screeching wind. Snowflakes landed on his face and stung his eyes.

Above, the men's laughter rang out. Volund howled in pain and rage.

And then he shut his eyes.

He had survived two years of servitude to the dvergar. Oh, he had known suffering. They had forged him from it like tempered steel. And if they had not broken him, neither would some worthless king.

9

DAYS GONE

Ten Years Ago

A year in the shadowed halls had toned his muscles, his body. More so, it had toned his mind and soul. As Dvalin had promised, they had visited nigh unto every torment imaginable upon him in an attempt to break him, to drive him to despair. Once, Dvalin had promised him if he begged for mercy he would be granted it. Volund had refused and could have sworn Dvalin looked on with pride, even as his slaves branded Volund's back with irons from the forge.

And Volund had not broken.

He could work a forge for days on end—as Dvalin often demanded. At thirteen winters, he could lift more than most men twice his age. And slowly, over the passing of moon after moon, the dvergar began to teach him their lore. For they understood the true nature of stones and metals and gems. All manner of precious things they knew, and bit by bit he began to know it too.

After working uncounted hours, Volund returned to his

chamber. Day and night meant less down here. He slept when he could. They had furnished him with a stone slab covered in furs. He'd thought he'd never sleep there, but after working himself bone weary he did. Every time he came here.

Tonight, though, Astrid lay under those furs, naked.

Not everything was suffering here. No, once they had decided Volund would not break, they began to offer him all the same indulgences—excesses really—they sated their own desires upon. When they ate, they feasted. When they drank, they drank themselves into a stupor. And the slaves they sometimes passed around. As he had been told, any slave he wished—male or female—was his to claim.

At first he had been too shy to do so, and the dvergar had mocked him for it. Dvalin's brother Durin had suggested Volund preferred having a dverg cock rammed up his arse. Soon, Volund had taken to sending for a girl. One time even, two girls at once. He had enjoyed that experience less than he expected, despite Dvalin's claims of taking on seven. Always, he asked their names. That was not a mistake he would ever repeat.

He slipped beneath the blankets beside Astrid and took her slowly. With a lot of practice, he'd found his bedmates actually seemed to enjoy his attentions. He liked Astrid. She was a cupbearer he'd first met two moons back. The dvergar discouraged attachment and had frowned when he'd favored one girl more than the next. They had not been kind to the object of his misguided affections. He was careful now, not growing too close. Not calling on any slave too often.

Dvalin told him their language had nine words for lust. It had no words for love. Not romantic love, at least, though the dvergar seemed to care a great deal about their children and lineages.

He groaned in release and held Astrid close.

And now the year was ending. His apprenticeship would be over any day now. Father would return and take him back to Kvenland. For the life of him, it was hard to decide how to feel about that. The worst suffering of his life had come in these dark, cold halls. But then, so too had he expanded his mind far beyond the dreams of other men. Enough to know more secrets remained just out of reach. He would return home the finest mortal smith in the North Realms. And yet, still far below the dvergar in his craft—at once a master, and a pale imitator.

A SLAVE WOKE Volund to tell him Dvalin had sent for him. Astrid was gone already. She never stayed. And he was not fool enough to ask. The dvergar did not have a word for love and they did not like to see aught that might be mistaken for it.

He found the dverg prince downing a mug of mead almost as large as his own head. Three other such mugs lay empty on the table before him. Volund waited for Dvalin to invite him to sit. The dverg belched then motioned for him to do so.

When he had settled, Dvalin waved to a slave to bring Volund a mug as well. Dverg mead was heady, and Volund still could not drain a full mug at once, though they kept asking him to practice. He took a long swig, wiped his mouth, then stared at Dvalin.

"Your father loiters outside our gates. Come to claim you, Volund."

This was goodbye then. A drunken send-off was the dverg custom, and they would not show any other form of remorse or regret. It was not their way. "I almost wish ... I had more time."

"Do you now?" Dvalin spit on the floor. "Few are given what they want in life. Such is the way of the World." It was his favorite aphorism. The dverg word for *cynicism* was the same as their word for *practicality*.

Volund shrugged. Dvalin was right, of course. Few got what they wanted.

"So." Dvalin belched. "Your father is a bastard prince of Kvenland. And your mother?"

Volund cocked an eyebrow at that. "I thought you didn't care about mortal lineages?"

"I don't. Fuck it." He motioned for another drink, and a slave girl—Astrid, he suddenly realized—brought it.

Volund let his eyes meet hers for the briefest of instants. Not so long Dvalin would notice. He hoped.

"You wish to stay in Nidavellir?"

What a dangerous question. Most of those invited to stay never left, for one reason or another. One had to be very careful about expressing one's wishes to the dvergar. They were wont to grant what was asked while arduously avoiding all that was desired. "I do not wish to become a host to a dverg spirit."

It had come as a shock to learn that was their true nature. Spirits without body in this Realm, who took mortal hosts. If the host was not willing, it had to be beaten down, his or her soul broken to allow for possession. Over time, they changed. Their bodies warped by the vaettir inside.

Dvalin snorted then waggled a calloused finger at him, as if acknowledging a well-played move. They loved their strategy games here. He and Dvalin had passed many hours in front of a tafl board. Dvalin always won. As did Durin and all the others he had played. "No. I think you would not be suited for it."

What in the fathomless dark of Svartalfheim did that mean?

"But," Dvalin said. "There is something inside you. Something that could be great, could be legendary. Perhaps with a bit more tempering."

Unpleasant as his "tempering" had been, some part of him almost longed for more. That probably meant he had a sickness in his head, if not his very soul. But that suffering had made him strong.

He leaned forward. "What would you have me do?"

IT WAS dark out when the great gates opened. Dark, and still the moonlight stung his eyes, seemed too bright after a year of naught but torches to see with.

His father rose from a crouch as Volund strode outside. "Gods, boy, I hardly recognize you." Father raced over and embraced him tightly.

The open display of such affection seemed off, a little alien. Despite that, Volund returned his father's embrace. How could he not? Some of the same guards watched him, nodding with approval. Yes, he had grown taller and much broader of shoulder. He knew that.

Volund greeted those guards he knew. They all congratulated him, spoke their empty praises. Somehow, he could feel the questions they wanted to ask about his time here. About what went on beyond the gates. The truth was, even were he inclined to share, they would not understand. Nidavellir might have been a dverg kingdom on Midgard, an imitation of their true world of Nidafjoll, and yet, despite lying *in* Midgard, it was not *of* Midgard. His people had no way to imagine the truths buried in the stones.

And no sign of his brothers. Shame.

He pulled away.

"We can leave at first light," his father said. "The braziers here keep the mist and vaettir at bay, so we're safe for now."

Volund grunted. "I must speak with you."

His father motioned him away from the camp, and Volund walked with him, until they stood in the shadow of one of the towers. The chill wind bothered him less than he'd have expected, though his father shuddered.

"They made me an offer," Volund said.

Confusion played out over his father's face. Confusion and perhaps ambition. The past year had given Volund time to wonder at his father's reasons for sending him in the first place. As a bastard son of the king, Wade would be given a comfortable life, but his legitimate brother stood to inherit everything. Did he hope for glory through the deeds of his son? For wealth? Or did he consider some more elaborate plot to take the throne when his own aging father passed? It was hard to tell. Volund had left his father a child—twelve winters though he'd had—and now looked at him with a man's eyes.

He had wished his brothers would be here to meet him. But maybe their presence would have made things harder on him.

Volund ran his fingers over the ice on the back of the tower. "They believe I have a gift, one they wish to nurture. They want to extend my apprenticeship."

His father nodded slowly, his lips working. "I have not brought more gold to offer."

Yes, there was that. The complexity of the offer. The

dvergar made their deals with twists unfathomable to a mortal mind. Sometimes Volund thought their games more elaborate than any match of tafl. Sometimes, he thought they just liked to wring suffering out of others. To watch them writhe like prey caught in a snare.

"They ask for no more gold, Father. In fact, they will return half your payment. But you must return exactly one year from today. Return even one day late, and all the gold is forfeit." Volund swallowed. Dvalin played for higher stakes than that, after all. "As am I."

"What?"

At the mention of the return of gold, his father's eyes had glittered. Now, his face fell and he was already shaking his head. True affection, or a show of it? Or perhaps the dvergar had infected him with their cynicism. *Practicality*. Volund supposed it didn't matter at the moment.

"There is much more I can learn." He could leave now. Go home with his father, meet his brothers. Suffer no further tortures in the darkness beneath the mountains.

He could leave it all behind.

And never know the greatest secrets. Always know he had turned back when but a few more steps into that darkness might have made him a legend.

"You *want* to take this deal?"

Volund held his peace a moment. "Yes." He did. Despite himself, he desired it. He *needed* it.

His father glanced back at the men, then rubbed his temples. Weighing the offer? To not only get his gold back, but get more training for his son? How could he turn it down?

And when he looked back at Volund, there was the answer. Father would never turn down such a chance. "I will return in one year, to the day."

10

AGILAZ

There were a lot of tracks in the fresh snow—men hunting through the woods around Vestborg. With the clear skies, maybe they did not know how close a fresh storm was drawing. Maybe they thought they could track their prey before it hit. That was certainly how Agilaz felt.

But while the Skaldun thegn and his men hunted a reindeer, Agilaz hunted them. They were too many—five men following one animal, and more like to scare it off than catch it. Fear kept men from wandering alone, especially in winter, as if numbers would protect them from a snowstorm. Agilaz had chosen to go alone this time. After Erik's betrayal, it seemed hard to trust any of the Hasding men. Besides, in this sort of hunt, there was more to lose than scaring away the game.

He crept among the spruces and pines, bow in hand. Men spoke in hushed voices, their whispers carrying farther than they probably expected. Agilaz had managed to track the reindeer and get ahead of it. It seemed the thegn's hunters were at least partly competent, because they had followed.

Maybe he should have just taken Hermod and left. Maybe an attempt to find Olrun like this was a waste of time, a pointless risk. He could probably still walk away. Slip off in the opposite direction, return and tell Hadding he'd had no chance to move against the Skaldun men. If the jarl bought it, he might let Agilaz take Hermod.

No. Damn, but no. He had a plan, and you had to stick to a plan or you had naught. He needed his wife. He needed her beautiful song. And his son needed a mother.

He slung the bow over his shoulder, then jumped up to catch a low-hanging branch. After pulling himself up onto it, he began to climb higher and higher into the tree. The forest here was dense, even in winter. Thick enough to conceal a man who could climb well. And Agilaz could.

Once he reached high enough, he swung one leg over the branch to steady himself. Then he unslung his bow and nocked an arrow. There was a definite pitfall to his plan. If they did spot him, he had very little ability to maneuver while in the tree. They would plant him full of arrows almost as easily as he would them. It meant he needed to be certain he made every shot count. He had a full quiver, but he was like to get no more than a dozen shots in.

The reindeer walked beneath him, but a few trees over. It raised its head as though it had his scent. That would only matter if the beast—

It bolted.

Damn it.

The hunting party came crashing through the trees a moment later, chasing after the fleeing deer. Running targets were harder. Not impossible though.

Agilaz lined up a shot at the farthest man. He had no idea who their leader was, but that was the one most likely to escape. He loosed. Even before it struck, he was already pulling another arrow.

His target pitched forward into the snow.

"What in Hel's—"

His second arrow took the speaker in the face.

"Take cover!" someone shouted.

Agilaz loosed at a man's chest, but he moved quickly, and it just grazed his arm. Dammit.

"There!"

And they had found him. It was a dozen feet down but ...

An arrow slammed into the trunk a foot from his face, quivering there.

Fuck it all. Agilaz leapt away from the tree, landing in a pile of snow. He rolled with it. Still, his legs felt numb from the impact. Grunting, he surged to his feet and dashed behind the tree. Another arrow struck it a heartbeat later.

He nocked again, stepped around, and loosed at the first target he saw. His shot caught an archer in the shoulder. The man dropped his bow, screaming, clutching the wound.

Two men left—one fresh, one wounded.

As he nocked another arrow, he peeked his head around. An arrow grazed his cheek and scraped the tree, flinging shards of bark in his eyes. Agilaz jerked backward. Yes, they were trying to flank him.

If they caught him between them—or if either of them got close enough to use those swords on their belts—the battle would not end in his favor.

He peeked again, but not with intention of seeing aught. The moment he heard a twang he took off running to the opposite side, then skidded behind another tree. He couldn't move fast enough in the snow. Blood was running down his cheek, pooling about his neck.

One of the men shouted a war cry. Snow crunched under his heels as he charged forward. His first and last mistake.

Agilaz dropped to one knee and spun on the charging man, an arrow flying even as he did so. It took the warrior in the gut. The man pulled up short, sword falling from his hand as he stared at his wound. It was the man he'd wounded before.

That left only a single healthy foe, and possibly the one with an arrow in his shoulder.

Spinning, he turned his eyes to the opposite side. His last healthy foe was indeed slipping between trees, trying to close in for a clear shot. Agilaz scrambled to keep the nearest tree between himself and the other archer.

The man did the same, slipping behind cover and loosing a single arrow. No shot from here.

The one with the gut wound was trying to rise. Tough bastard. Agilaz planted another shot in his chest, and he fell.

"Let's settle this like men," the last one shouted.

"So be it."

His foe tossed the bow aside and pulled a sword off his shoulder. Holding it before him, he advanced out into the open.

Agilaz stepped out too. Then he launched an arrow at his attacker. The man reeled, falling backward. He tried to rise, to charge, but Agilaz put another arrow in his chest. He collapsed in the snow.

One last man, and he might already be unconscious from blood loss. Still, he had to be found.

"You cheated ..." the man he'd just shot said.

Agilaz cast a glance over his shoulder. "Men can use bows."

He wiped the blood from his cheek. One more man to kill, and one of these had to be the thegn. If Hadding was right, it meant Vestborg would fall, the Skalduns retreating without their leader. And returning the border fort to Hasding hands.

11

VOLUND

*B*y the time they pulled Volund up, his legs had gone so numb he could do naught but collapse on the platform. Nidud's men had to drag him back into the great hall by his shoulders. His head throbbed from the blood that had rushed to it. He'd have expected his thoughts would blur from deathchill, but instead they had sharpened into the clarity of a dream. A dream which, immersed within, might strike one as truth even as one knew it for illusion.

In his dream, Volund was not a man at all. He was a whisper, stalking the night as though one of the vaettir, lurking in darkness. The cold had seeped into him so deeply he no longer felt it—he became it. And the freezing wind had ceased to bother him, for he knew with certainty revenge would be his.

The feeble torchlight within the great hall failed to banish the shadows. This place, this dvergar hall, had not been built with the intention of welcoming the light that Mankind—in their self-delusion—thought would protect them. Light was a temporary disturbance in the natural state of things. All fires would one day burn out, the last flames flicker to nothingness. Darkness was the truth.

And so, though his lips must have been cracked and blue, he smiled at Nidud as they dropped him at the king's feet. The king raised an eyebrow while the queen shifted in her throne, her eyes looking anywhere but at him. Beside them stood a thick-armed man, his face soot-smudged and scowling.

Nidud cleared his throat, the sound of it thick with phlegm. "Now, smith, you will show us the extent of your craft."

Volund wanted to laugh, but his voice might well break and leave him looking pathetic. Instead, he kept his smile. It must infuriate the king.

"My finest smith has crafted a suit of mail from dverg steel." The king nodded at the heavy man beside him. "He claims such armor will make my sons impervious in battle. If it does, he shall have his weight in silver."

The other smith nodded.

Volund ignored him, keeping his eyes locked on the king.

"You will make a sword to match, one capable of scoring even such mail as Amelias has forged."

"Why would I do that?" His voice had become a raspy, violent sound. He might have hated it, if it had not left everyone in the hall squirming.

"Because if you do not, you have no use to me and shall spend the rest of your days hanging from that platform. Ravens will feast on your eyes and pick clean your bones. And no man shall ever again speak your name. The sum of your life will mean less than that of a dog's." The king spoke flatly, as though discussing what he'd prefer to eat for the night meal.

Volund had to admit Nidud gave a remarkable display of calm authority. The threat, spoken so plainly, gained more credence. And if Nidud did kill him here, he might never again find Altvir. And find her he must. She was his ... light. Did he still need the light? Darkness had begun to feel comfortable. But she had given him the only peace, the only love in his life.

"I will forge your sword."

THE SMITH, Amelias, accompanied Volund as they descended deeper and deeper into the mountain. Were it not for the half dozen guards, Volund might have slain the man. They had, after all, removed his chains so that he might work the forge. And how could he not welcome the chance to once more craft in a deep forge of the dvergar? There, the true extent of his talent could be manifest and give birth to wonders the likes of which men would not imagine. Oh, this fool smith beside him did not know, could not know the secrets. Could not even fathom the depths of his own ignorance.

Long stone steps took them into the heart of the mountain. Eventually, these steps opened into a cavern. In the hidden recesses above, bats laired among the stalactites. Volund could feel them, lurking in the shadows. If they were here, they had some egress from the cavern, some way to hunt. Pity such an escape must lie so high above him. Unlike Altvir, Volund could not take the form of a swan and simply fly away.

The stairs leveled into a great bridge spanning an underground lake. The bridge ran several hundred feet to a rocky island. Halfway across, a guard-post stood, great iron gears attaching to chains on the bridge. The dvergar had built an extending bridge here. They had such defenses in Nidavellir, too. They spoke little of what foes might warrant their fear, but he suspected that in addition to Niflungar and the Vanir, they feared the other vaettir. The dvergar despised the radiant liosalfar and rightfully mistrusted the shadowy svartalfar. No spirit was wont to trust one of another world, after all. In this world, they competed for mortal hosts and for footholds to secure passage between the Realms.

Mankind, of course, had no idea how perilous Midgard's position truly was. Perhaps the Vanir alone kept the horrors at bay. But then, they rarely ventured forth from their islands anymore, or such was the talk among the dvergar, at least. The Vanir had lost their interest in the dealings of Men, so threats from beyond once again had begun to stir. Even the dvergar spoke of spreading their kingdom, of over-mastering the whole of the North Realms.

The bridge was already extended, leading all the way to the island, upon which rose a great rocky pillar. Faint fire-light shone from a massive doorway in this pillar, one three times the height of a man. A deep forge.

Volund could not keep the hurry from his step. The forge called to him, whispered that he might work his craft here. And in those whispers there was something more, some hint of a secret he had not quite grasped. But he would.

Amelias and the guards paused at the edge of the island. Those soldiers even leveled spears at Volund as he glanced back at them.

"The king gives you a fortnight to forge your sword." Yes, his voice was thick with disdain, haughty and proud. And underneath that, a hint of worry. He knew he would lose his place as Nidud's prized smith. When Volund succeeded—and if this forge was stocked with adamant, he would surely make a blade capable of scoring Amelias's armor—the king would know the man as a pretender.

"It will take nine days," Volund said. "In nine days, the king shall have a blade worthy of a great name. And in nine days you, smith, shall fall at my feet and beg me to share my arts."

Amelias spat into the lake and turned. Despite his eagerness to explore the forge, Volund watched them go. They returned to the guardhouse. Within, they must have activated the levers, for the great stone bridge began to recede away from the island, the grinding of stone on stone echoing throughout the cavern.

He might well swim out there. The lake waters were undoubtedly cold, but he had survived the punishing winds up on the mountain. Still, if they trusted the lake to contain him, he had to believe the dvergar had some defenses there as well. Serpents bred for the purpose, most likely.

No, he would not swim from here. Regardless, he could no longer resist the call of the deep forge. He half-dashed the long path to the entryway. Once there, he fell to stillness. The forge within was bigger than the halls of many kings, lined with numerous fire pits. At its heart lay a furnace that could rage with primeval heat.

Slowly, he walked the place. Stores of iron, silver, even gold and—yes, adamant—lined the walls in bins. Small wonder that Nidud had lived so long then. The wealth of this place must have bought him as many mercenaries as he could ever want. If he needed more, he'd simply come down for a few more nuggets of gold.

Some of the bins were empty, long plundered of their

precious ores. That the dvergar had left any was a testament to how suddenly they must have ...

Volund paused over one of the bins. Impossible. That red-gold, just lying there. Orichalcum? Only a few nuggets remained now, but the men here had left it. By the fathomless dark of Svartalfheim, the fools must have mistaken it for copper. He ought not to be surprised. Probably they had never seen, maybe never even heard of a metal so precious. And next to iron and gold and adamant, who would care about a few lumps of copper? Volund gingerly lifted a hunk of it out and drew it up to his face. Imbeciles had no idea they sat upon the greatest treasure imaginable. He licked the ore. Yes, that bittersweet taste was unmistakable.

A rough shudder overtook him.

Forge it.

The whispers had grown clearer. If the shadows spoke to him, then in truth the darkness the dvergar had planted in him had encompassed his mind. And if so, perhaps there was no longer any escape from it.

Forge it.

Volund grasped another chunk of orichalcum. Did he even still seek escape? This ignorant, petty king thought to imprison him, but unknowingly, had gifted Volund with a chance to make something that had become mere legend even among the dvergar.

You know the workings.

Yes. He had seen the records among his mentor's things, the ancient art all but lost. Long had he wondered why Dvalin might have let him glimpse such forbidden and nigh forgotten lore. Now he knew. The ancient dverg must have had some foreboding of this moment, some premonition that one day, his human apprentice might do as he himself had done long ago.

In the darkness of a deep forge, Dvalin and his brothers had wrought nine runeblades of orichalcum. Nine swords with the power to change a man's destiny, to strike any foe, to fell even the most monstrous of beasts.

Nine blades, most lost.

And now, Volund would forge a tenth.

12

DAYS GONE

Ten Years Ago

The dvergar liked their drink, especially ale and mead. They consumed vast draughts of both and mocked Volund for never being able to match them.

He thought that perhaps it was good-natured enough. For he had been scourged some few hours ago, endured it without screaming. Durin had brought him sapphire shrooms then. The hallucinogenic mushrooms dulled pain and enticed visions. Volund oft saw things he might rather have not. At least at first. Figures moving in the darkness, speaking in whispers. Tongues that seemed older than the stars. The ancient dverg tongue was derived from the older-still Supernal speech of vaettir who had existed long before the time of Mankind and would no doubt linger when humanity had finally faded back to dust.

The dvergar cultivated sapphire shrooms throughout Nidavellir and named them for the streaks of blue that ran through the fungus. Too much was toxic, especially to mortals. He had found that out after eating several raw. He spent the next three days heaving and squirting shits until he thought his insides would burst out.

Today though, they had given him a distilled draught. And when his head had begun to clear, Dvalin and Durin had invited him to drink with them. The princes of Nidavellir had a private hall. The king—whom Volund had rarely seen—had sired a great many sons on a great many women. Some of those sons, like Dvalin, had won great renown in their own right.

Durin belched again and slammed his mug on the table. "Tell me, boy. If you could make aught in the world, any craft, what would you forge?"

"Another runeblade." Volund spoke without thinking, without even realizing he *had* wanted such a thing. Orichalcum was so rare that no one had forged another runeblade in centuries.

Durin chuckled.

Dvalin, however, fixed him with a level gaze. "Do you know why we made them?"

Volund shook his head. "No, Master." The obvious answer seemed to be "because you could." That answer might have gotten him whipped or beaten.

"My brothers and I, the three of us, forged one blade for each of the nine kingdoms of men in the North Realms, those you now call the Old Kingdoms. One blade to grace the hand of a champion. Within these blades, we bound a fell curse that all Men should desire them, should kill for them and with them. And should they ever fail to honor us, the blades would twist their urds and bring ruination to all they loved."

Durin drummed his fingers on the table. "And for working this Art, we lay in a stupor, weakened for a moon, it seemed. We forged the souls of nine sacrifices into each blade. And the blades themselves—we used nigh all the orichalcum we had."

Eighty-one people slain for this, their very souls beaten into the metal. Volund frowned. "Why? Why create such works for mortal Men?"

Dvalin looked at his brother, before spitting. "The princes of the Old Kingdoms were descended from the sons of Halfdan the Old. And he was not exactly a mortal Man."

What did that mean? Perhaps it was the ale, or the lingering effects of the sapphire shrooms, but none of this made sense to him. "How could he be aught else?"

"He was a half-alf, boy. And so his lineage carried with it ancient power from beyond the Mortal Realm."

Volund's mouth hung open a moment before he could form a question. He had not known such a thing was possible. "Liosalf or svartalf?"

Dvalin tugged on his beard. "No one was quite certain. In either case, we were willing to risk a great deal to control such a power."

"They are more powerful than dvergar?"

"They are older."

Durin rose, swaying, and toppled back down into his seat. "We forged the runeblades for a purpose, boy. We could not make more even had we the will to do so."

Most of those runeblades had been lost during the fall of the Old Kingdoms. They became things of legend. Durin had once claimed Frey's flaming sword was one of their number, was his own work. But there was not enough orichalcum for such a craft now, and had there been, the dvergar would not have granted it to Volund.

He would never make such glorious works.

13

VOLUND

*V*olund blew flecks off the sword, the last of the runes etched into the blade. The shards of metal flew about the forge, carried on an unseen and unfelt wind as the shadows seemed to laugh in victory. Perhaps the shadows had been drawing him to this place his entire life.

Urd.

Once, drunken and fey, Dvalin had spoken of the Norns. Beings he claimed were neither quite mortal nor vaettir, who wove the urd of both. Perhaps the Norns were the shadows speaking to Volund now.

The blade, as it was, was stronger and sharper than any ever forged by a man; of that Volund had no doubt. And though he did not consider himself a sorcerer in name, he knew enough of the Art to carve the runes of power. All dverg smiths were, in effect, dabblers in the Art. The spirit he had bound to the blade was hungry and, without a soul to sate it, might break free, unbind the enchantments, and wreak unfathomable havoc upon the men of this hold.

The thought brought a bitter satisfaction with it. But he, the one who dared evoke the angered vaettr, would no doubt fall victim first. And what was his vengeance on Nidud were he not there to see despair overcome the wicked king? No, Volund's revenge needed time to temper.

Nine days. Yes, the prescribed time for the forging of a great work. He had named the time he needed on a whim— or so he thought. Perhaps that too had been urd, for a runeblade demanded nine days. No less and no more.

Volund had not had time to craft a fitting scabbard for such a blade. Perhaps he would do so next. He ought to work golden threads into it, perhaps even in a dragon motif. Men feared dragons above nigh all else and not without reason, if the dvergar spoke true. Not even they wished to disturb ancient serpents. Only the alfar seemed to hold more foreboding for them.

Stone scraping on stone echoed from the cavern outside. Volund smiled. It seemed Amelias had taken him at his word that he would need but nine days. Or perhaps the smith doubted him and came to mock work he might think unfinished.

Sword flat on his shoulder, he strolled out from the forge to meet the man. It was not Amelias who crossed the bridge, however, but the thegn Thakkrad. The man paused at the island's threshold, eyes darting back and forth between Volund and the blade.

And here, delivered onto his doorstep, the very man who had first wronged him. This worm had dared piss upon him like he was some filthy peasant and not the son of a king. Volund did not have nine souls to bind to the blade, but perhaps one would do.

The thegn shook his head. "What in Hel's trench happened to you?"

Not quite the question Volund had expected.

"Wasn't his hair auburn?" one of the guards behind Thakkrad said.

What were these cretins on about now? Volund grabbed a lock of his hair from beside his face to examine it. Indeed, it had turned a mix of gray and black. Perhaps it was caked in soot. Or perhaps working the Art had changed him. His mortal form was not as suited for such violations of nature as one possessed by a vaettr. Such workings had incapacitated Dvalin and his brothers. And yet he did not feel weakened or aged. No, he felt strong, invigorated. Enough that he might charge those swine on the bridge and cut them down, feed them to his blade.

Not them.

Yes, perhaps the shadows spoke truth. If he tried such a thing, he might kill two or three or even four of them. But he was not the warrior his brothers were. Eventually, Nidud's men would cut him down, runeblade or no.

So he must yet temper his vengeance.

Forcing a smile he hoped looked much like the grin of a saber-toothed cat, he held the blade out before him, flat so the guards could see his work. "Nine days are passed. Has the king not come to see what his actions have purchased?"

Thakkrad spat. "The king does not deign to come all the way down to you, smith. You walk up to him."

Volund sneered. As if the aged Nidud *could* climb down here. The decrepit fool's heart would give out before he reached halfway, probably saving them all a great deal of trouble. "Then lead the way."

The guards back away, spears leveled. They feared him. Six men, and they feared him. It was rich, a feeling he could quite get used to.

IN THE GREAT HALL, the king and queen sat once again, this time flanked by two young men, the youngest only a few winters past the age of manhood. Both were standing in silent bluster, trying to look important. Perhaps all young men did so. Volund's coming of age had meant the beginning of his apprenticeship to Dvalin. Who had these whelps trained under? Certainly not their father, who was well past his fighting days. Thakkrad, perhaps. Yes, the favored thegn of the king no doubt trained his boys. For all Volund knew, he had sired them as well. It must prove hard for the faltering king to get it up, after all.

Hold your tongue.

There was wisdom in silence, in letting men wonder what one knew, what one thought. And how odd to think these men seemed not to hear the shadows, for they spoke so clearly now. Warnings and wisdoms both.

The guards escorted him to the center of the hall, then backed away, just out of spear's reach. They seemed disinclined to let him get too close. Not quite total fools then.

Volund hefted the sword, at which the spearmen took up fighting stances. He ignored them, focused on Nidud. "I give you Mimung. Such a blade you have never known."

"You named an unproven sword?" The voice came from the left side of the hall as Amelias stalked forward. Despite his brave words, his steps lacked confidence. And he was clad in a suit of dark mail, one quite likely forged from adamant, if perhaps a little ineptly.

"He now has the chance to prove it," Nidud said. "Do as I have commanded and score that armor, and all will call you the finest smith in the North Realms."

Volund cast a wary glance at the king. "In all Midgard, save the dvergar themselves."

"His arrogance knows no bounds," Amelias shouted.

Needlessly raising his voice in a place of such acoustics only spoke to his doubt. Surely he hoped to convince himself more than anyone else. To make himself think the sword would not harm him through that armor.

And true, adamant chain would stop most blades without suffering so much as a scratch. Mimung was not most blades. The king had granted Volund yet another gift.

"Very well, great smith Volund," Nidud said. "If you manage to actually draw blood, your name shall be heralded as the greatest smith in Midgard. Save the dvergar. But if you fail to scratch that armor, skalds will tell of your misery in hushed tones in the dark night. Your urd shall be the greatest fear of men across the North Realms. The name Volund shall come to be a curse of suffering beyond compare."

Volund bowed. "I accept your challenge." He turned to Amelias. "Come to me, smith. Let us see if I can draw blood from beneath that mail."

The smith looked to his king, who made no acknowledgment. Then, to his credit, he strode forward with an admirable attempt at bravado. The spearmen backed another step away, giving him room to swing.

"I trust you have tested this mail?" Volund asked. "It turned a blade once or twice?"

"A blade, an axe, a spear point." Amelias spread his arms, giving Volund a chance to inspect his work.

He did so, taking a step forward and nodding. "Well. I can see you've done your best." He grasped Mimung in both hands and took a sudden stroke downward at an angle. The blade struck Amelias on the clavicle and sheared through mail, flesh, and bone, then bit into the man's spine.

And there, unfortunately for Amelias, it did its true work. The spirit within latched onto the smith's soul, sucking hungrily on the dying feast. The man's life ended in an instant, but a rush built through Volund's arm, an energy unlike aught he had ever felt. It drained Amelias of all he was, until even Volund could swear he'd gorged himself on a solstice feast. And the blade pulled from him as well, eating little bits of his own life force to bind that spirit in perpetuity.

Volund fell to his knees as he yanked the blade free from the corpse. He gasped, panting. It was like every bit of strength had been sucked out of him, and he felt as numb as he had when they brought him in from the platform. The Art had taken more toll on him than he'd expected. This must have been what Durin had meant by the drain of it. And still, a grim satisfaction filled him.

Screams and shouts rang through the hall. Actually, it sounded like a woman had retched somewhere. Volund wanted to laugh.

Something hard and swift slapped him between the shoulder blades and he fell forward. Mimung clattered away, and another soldier grabbed it before he could rise. No, not just a soldier—Thakkrad, eyeing the blade hungrily.

Volund struggled to his knees, watching the royal pair. The queen had a hand over her mouth, eyes wide. Nidud, though, looked thoughtful. Maybe even pleased. Yes, he too had become steeped in the darkness of this place. It had seeped into him and changed him, strengthened him. Volund was wrong in his first impression. Nidud was not some weak old man. Not at all.

By his side, the youngest of the sons was cackling as though it was the best show he'd ever seen. Perhaps fortunate for all the boy was not next in line for the throne. The child had the cruelty of a dverg or even a svartalf.

"Thakkrad," Nidud said. "See that the blade reaches my son Otwin on the front lines."

The thegn stared at the blade so long Volund wondered if he would challenge the king for it. Instead, he bowed at last.

The queen's trembling eyes were locked on Volund's. Yes, she feared him. The air was so thick with it he could drink it like mead. So he smiled at her, the kind of smile that promised her the fulfillment of every nightmarish thought in her head.

She looked away then, burying her face at her husband's ear and whispering.

Nidud grunted, then nodded. "Thakkrad."

The thegn had already headed for the hall's entrance, but turned back at his king's call.

"Our smith has outdone even his own reputation. It seems prudent to hold onto such a valuable man."

Thakkrad grinned. "I'll take him back to the island. He can make armor to stand up to the blade."

"Yes do. But before that, it seems prudent to ensure he won't try to leave our employ. Cut the hamstring on his right leg. Use Mimung."

Volund jumped to his feet only to be shoved back down by three guards. "What! You cannot! You dare not!"

Rough hands shoved him forward, bent him double.

"As my king commands," Thakkrad said.

Someone held Volund's neck down. He couldn't see the thegn approaching. But he could feel it. The man stalking closer. The cruelty in him saturated the air and made shadows dance before Volund's eyes.

"No! No!"

A chill blade like a razor settled on the back of his thigh.

Gods, where were the voices? Had they abandoned him

now? What was he to do? There must be some way he could—

The blade bit deep, slicing through tendon like bread. So sharp it took a heartbeat longer for the pain to hit. And then the pain of his wound crashed over him like a falling mountain.

14

DAYS GONE

Nine Years Ago

*T*hey had forced him to walk over acid. A thin layer of the substance, used for etching metal, spread across a depression in the floor. The dvergar had said the worst part would be the acrid smell of his bubbling feet. They were wrong, of course. The worst part was the agony. Waves of it, a raging torrent of pain that constantly threatened to pitch him forward. Had he fallen, the acid might have eaten away at his arms, chest, face.

And so he remained on his feet, screaming with each step. He did not cry the names of the gods, nor curse the dvergar, at least not that he recalled. It seemed rather an incoherent primal scream of denial.

Durin treated him afterward, as always. In this case, the dverg spread a cooling salve over his feet while he lay abed. They had given him a draught of sapphire shrooms that had eased his pain, but left the room spinning, shadows playing a musical dance. The dverg had the gentleness of a mountain goat, his coarse hands nigh painful enough to negate any benefit of the salve, at least at first.

When he had finish slathering the paste over Volund's feet, Durin sat back and shrugged. "Ought to do you."

"What exactly was this lesson supposed to teach me, anyway?"

"If you have to ask, I'd say you didn't fucking learn it." Durin spat to make his point.

Oh, Volund had understood. Dvalin had caught him boasting of his skills to some of the other dvergar. Boasting, in fact, that even some of them had become jealous of him. And it was the truth. Their eyes watched him with envy.

"Not to mock the dvergar," Volund finally mumbled.

"Eat a fucking stone bubble, shit-for-brains. The point was your fucking pride's apt to cost you more than it buys."

"What do we have but our pride? Do you not regale me often enough with tales of your noble lineage?"

The dverg was wont to carry on about his father, Modsognir, but did not oft boast of his own accomplishments—except for his greatest works, the runeblades.

Volund listened, of course. To do otherwise would not only have proved rude, it would have denied him one of his few chances to learn more about the dvergar beyond Nidavellir. For sometimes Durin even spoke of Nidafjoll, the world these spirits hailed from.

Now though, the dverg shook his head. "Pride, yes. It is a failing they gave us."

"What?"

Durin settled back on the floor, groaning. "The legends say, long before the mist, the powers of Sun and Darkness warred. Did you know that?"

"I know no truths from before the mists. You speak of the worlds in the Spirit Realm?"

Durin spat. "Fucking liosalfar. The svartalfar fought them, raised us up from the rocks like maggots. Or so they told us. Sent us to fight their enemies. And the liosalfar cursed us, made the sun itself our enemy. There is no pride quite like that of the alfar. And for it, we were twice brought low."

The room was spinning, twisting with the effects of the sapphire shrooms. Had Durin gone, left him?

The dverg grabbed both sides of Volund's face with rocky palms. "Take care with your own pride, boy. You are thick with it, and one day it will cost you more than you know."

VOLUND SPENT PERHAPS HALF a moon in his convalescence. Some number of the dvergar visited him often enough, drank with him, until the day he could walk on his own. Then they expected him to return to the feast hall and carry on as if naught had happened. They did not need to tell him they expected this. He knew. Such was the way of the World.

Dvalin, in fact, said naught more of the incident. Perhaps to him it was but one more pain, humiliation, or other tempering of his student.

And Volund supposed it was. He hobbled around in pain for many days as Durin's salve regrew the ruined skin on his feet. The dvergar, of course, were damned to hobble around in pain for all eternity. No matter how fine a host they took, always the body would twist and warp out of alignment. If a human host were slowly transformed into a rough facsimile of a vaettr's true nature, Volund oft had to wonder how hideous these creatures must then appear in their own world. Not that he would ever be able to see their true forms.

After a feast, he returned to his chamber to find a girl there, but not one he had sent for. Indeed, it took him far longer than it ought have to recognize her.

"You. The one from the camp below here."

His first. He'd thought of her sometimes. He could remember the feel of her tiny breasts in his hands, yet no matter how tightly he closed his eyes he couldn't quite picture her face. And here she was, changed a bit in the past two winters. But definitely the same.

All those times imagining meeting her again, and now his tongue wouldn't work.

The girl nodded. "Your brother sent me."

Volund had to roll her words around in his mind to make sense of them. "Which brother?"

Damn fool question. The better question might have been to ask what his brother was doing here at all. Or why he'd send a slave girl to meet Volund. Or what her name was —the question he had wrestled with the past two years.

"Long brown hair and a scruffy beard. But he had another with him."

Slagfid. And with Agilaz, perhaps? So his year had ended, then.

"What did he … What's going on?"

The girl pressed herself close and Volund, despite his best intentions, suddenly found his arms around her. She stiffened at his caress, though, and whispered in his ear sternly.

"Yesterday your father came to find you. There was an avalanche on the way. Your father was buried in it."

Volund shoved the girl away. "What in the fathomless darkness of Svartalfheim! You spout lies."

She shook her head and motioned for him to lower his voice. "I am sorry for your loss, truly I am. Your brother plans to come here tomorrow and explain things to *them*."

Eyes shut, Volund shook his head. Based on the look on the girl's face, she knew as well as he did. *They* did not understand human excuses. The dvergar did not care to understand much of any such matters.

No, Dvalin's words. If Wade himself did not return ... tomorrow, gods! Already tomorrow? If Volund's father did not come here himself, the gold and Volund himself were forfeit. He backed away from her and slumped down onto the stone shelf that served as his bed.

In two years, he had learned many times more than another man might learn in a lifetime. But he could *not* remain here. There remained the very real possibility that Dvalin or his kin had engineered that avalanche. The dvergar did exert some measure of control over rock and stone when they were so inclined. They could move through it, send it tumbling one way or the next.

Even had Dvalin not arranged something like that, what urd would befall Volund were he to remain here? Host to a dverg spirit? Dvalin had once said he was not suited for that, though why he could not imagine. And if not, then what? Nidavellir would own him in truth, perhaps make him a slave. Perhaps something even worse than that.

He rose. No. He would not allow himself to meet such an end. His father had died for him, and Volund would grieve once he had won his freedom. But right now, his brothers were about to risk *their* lives on a vain hope of saving him. And he had to get to them before that.

On his wall hung a sword he had forged some moons back. Made from adamant. One of the finest masterpieces he had ever laid eyes on, though it was no runeblade. Even Dvalin had granted it grudging approval and let him keep it.

Volund snatched the sword and slung it over his shoulder, then grabbed the girl's hand. "Come. There is another exit."

He led her through the tunnels of Nidavellir, unable to shake the feeling that their every step echoed twice as loud as it ought. They passed slaves and dvergar both, but neither seemed to pay him any mind. Like his dvergar masters, Volund was known to take slave girls along with him often enough throughout the day. Perhaps that aided him now.

They descended into a tunnel with stairs that ran for a long distance before leveling out. He dare not speak here, where his voice would echo. Nor was this a place he was meant to be without permission. The tunnel led to a secret entrance, one used to bring in small amounts of supplies or the occasional new slave. Dvalin had had him retrieve some goats delivered here for a feast, eight, maybe nine moons back. The dverg had probably only told Volund about the place because he was too drunk to remember who to send.

At the tunnel's end, atop a walkway, stood a single snoring guard before a thick iron door. The lever below the walkway opened the door by chain pulleys, but there was no way to operate it without making noise.

Sometimes, a man was left with no good options. In such times, one had to choose the best of the bad options. Such was the way of the World. Volund slipped his sword from its sheath and slowly began to creep up the slope toward the sleeping dverg.

"Fucking stone bubbles, boy!"

Volund froze, cringing at Durin's shout from the lower landing. The guard in front sputtered awake, reaching for his spear.

Damn it, and damn Durin for following him. Without even looking back Volund swung, cleaving into the dverg's head. His blade clanked off the helm but slid down, biting through eye and nose and mouth. The dverg fell, clutching his ruined face.

Sword high, Volund turned now. Durin seemed to melt out of the stone. He stood behind the girl, one hand on her throat. She was a hair taller than the dverg, but Volund could see his face, his hard, disappointed eyes.

"You have no idea what you've done."

"Maimed that poor host and inconvenienced the spirit possessing him." Volund leapt off the ledge and fell six feet or so to land in front of Durin. "Release her. She has naught to do with this."

"You *care*? You're still too human, aren't you? And Dvalin thought he got it out of you. You never heard what I was trying to tell you, boy. Well, you care about this bitch?" Durin stepped back into the wall. The stone pooled and folded around him, letting him pass. The girl, it stopped cold. She slammed into the rock with a sickening crack that splattered her skull against it.

"No!"

The body slowly slid down the wall.

"Damn you, Durin! Why?"

The dverg stepped out of the wall where he had entered, rock flowing around him like water. "Because you are not supposed to get attached. Not like that. And because you must be punished for your temerity. I warned you about the cost of pride." The dverg now drew his own sword, circling around Volund.

"I wonder," Volund said, sparing at glance at the exit. "What time is it?"

"What?"

Volund kicked the lever. At once, the door began to recede into the ceiling, pulled up by the chains.

Durin shrieked as rays of sunlight poured through the base of the door. Volund used his momentary distraction to race up the slope. The guard was trying to rise. Volund hacked through his throat and then rolled under the door.

Outside, the sun was high. Bright. Too bright, it stung his eyes and felt like it burned his skin. His momentum carried him into the snow, and he tumbled down the steep path. End over end he fell, barely holding on to his sword, pitching forward before finally landing in a snow drift.

Gasping, world spinning, he tried to sit. Instead, he fell over sideways. For a time he lay there, panting, feeling the sun bake his skin.

He had never asked her name. He had intended to, had run it through his mind as they walked. He just thought they shouldn't talk until they had reached freedom.

And Frey's flaming sword. He'd killed a dverg. Or killed his host, at least. For that they would hunt him. Not now, not in daylight. He looked up. Morning still, which meant he had a very small time to move. To put as much distance between himself and the gates of Nidavellir as ...

His brothers. They were probably still in the slave camp. And when the sun set, they would be the ones to pay for his crimes.

Volund pushed himself up. Dvalin was right. The dverg had tempered him. He had created a man who could push beyond mortal limits, keep going despite pain, fatigue, hunger, or despair. And right now, Volund was going to need that.

PART II

Year 97, Age of Vingethor
End of Winter

15

SLAGFID

*T*hey had spent two moons chasing ghosts. The Niflungar did not engage them, despite Slagfid's best efforts. They vanished into the mists of their goddess, only to once again sweep away a man or a woman. Sometimes whole families.

And so King Frothi had paid their tribute, though it had nigh crippled his kingdom. Kelda took it hard, as a personal insult. But they could not move well in winter, and so they passed their nights watching over the town. Great patrols of ten, twelve men, each bearing a torch. The town consisted of nine thatch-roofed longhouses and the king's own great house, plus outlying fields and work houses. It was a lot to patrol. Still, no more families vanished. Slagfid wished he could attribute it to his diligence, but he knew it had only happened because Frothi had met their demands.

More moons passed then, one by one. And there was stillness. Even the patrols had ended long since.

Now though, winter had broken. And a new emissary had come to the court. The man had refused to enter the king's hall and so stood out in the square. He appeared just after sunset, demanding Frothi attend him.

Slagfid stood at one side of the hall, while Kelda stood beside her father. The king stared at the emissary, a man who had not even lowered the hood of his cloak. Indeed, mist writhed about his feet, coiling like a nest of serpents.

"Speak then," Frothi said. "What do you wish now?"

"Each kingdom in Reidgotaland is to pay us tribute equal to their king's weight in gold."

Slagfid had to bite his tongue to keep from chuckling at that. The lean winter had not worn away all of Frothi's over-sized gut. His people would be paying a fair bit more than the average kingdom. And it seemed the question they had all feared was answered—the Niflungar would indeed expect their tribute annually.

"How dare you?" Frothi fumbled with his own sword on his back. "Do you think you can bleed us dry? That we will simply fawn over you like some southern weaklings?"

At the king's motion, every other warrior readied their weapons. Including Slagfid. For once, he could see the foe before him.

With a battle cry, Kelda threw herself at the Niflung emissary. The man whipped his cloak around in front of her, and she stumbled, choking on a sudden blanket of mist. The shieldmaiden dropped her blade and fell to her knees, clutching her throat. Even as she fell, the sorcerer caught her wrist. She gasped, her face losing all color.

Slagfid charged forward an instant before the king. He swung at the sorcerer's wrist. The man released Kelda and twisted again, stepping behind Slagfid. Immediately Slagfid spun, using his momentum to continue his swing. His sword met the mist as though he had tried to swing it through a curtain of water. The resistance slowed his blow and his enemy danced away again.

The princess had fallen over, clutching her wrist where the sorcerer had touched her. Her cries of agony meant she was breathing, though.

Men raced after the Niflung, chasing him into the mist gathered between houses. Slagfid glanced back and forth between Kelda and the other men.

"Kill him!" Frothi bellowed, then knelt to help his daughter.

Yes, Slagfid had an oath to uphold. He raced into the mist himself, pausing only to grab a torch. He almost stumbled over the corpses littering that alley. Three men lay dead. Friends, men he had patrolled beside, drank with.

Slagfid waved the torch in front of him, but the alley appeared empty. He crouched to examine the bodies. One had turned blue, ice seeming to spread from a handprint around his throat. Poor Arvid. The other two had been cut down with a blade. If the sorcerer needed to use a sword, he was not all-powerful.

Once, Slagfid had asked his sword instructor how to fight a sorcerer. The man had fixed him with a level gaze and told him he had two options, neither good. The first— run and hide, and pray to any god who would listen the sorcerer did not find him. The second—fall to his knees and beg the sorcerer for mercy. But then, those who touched the Art were not known for their mercy.

Neither option would serve him this night.

Torch held before him, sword ready, Slagfid advanced into the mist. It had grown so thick it felt almost like a physical impediment, a wall pushing back against him, if only a bit. Whispers thick with ancient hatred sounded all around him.

"Njord," he whispered. "Grant me strength to uphold my oath."

A silhouette moved before him. Slagfid lunged forward and struck. The figure twisted to the side and again vanished into nothingness. Damn it. The torch banished the mist as his foe drew nigh, but not enough of it. Sunrise was too far away. This Hel-worshipping Niflung could probably kill the whole damn town before the first rays of dawn drove him from here.

That hissing mist. It mocked him.

A man screamed somewhere to his right.

Slagfid grimaced. He had promised Njord deaths, and he was going to deliver. "Forgive me," he mumbled. Then he flung the torch onto the roof of the house to his right. The snows had mostly melted, and the thatch caught almost immediately. In the space of a few heartbeats, the flames spread, erupting over the house. The mist evaporated, seeming almost to hiss in pain as the fire raged. Other vapors retreated like an animal from the flame.

The dancing figure appeared, cutting down another warrior. He saw Slagfid then and raced back toward the curtain of mist. Slagfid charged him, slamming into the sorcerer with his shoulder. The pair of them tumbled to the ground. Rather than try to gain his feet, Slagfid punched the Niflung in his face. The cowl fell away revealing the face of a man—albeit one with runes marked on it. Slagfid punched him again. Sorcerer or no, his nose shattered under the attack. Blood splattered over the man's face.

Slagfid rolled off him and rose, sword in hand. The sorcerer lunged for his own blade. Not fast enough. Slagfid's sword bit into the man's skull, shattering it in a mess of blood and brains. To be certain, Slagfid hacked away again and again. Gods only knew what it took to kill a sorcerer. Panting, he lifted the corpse by the hair and swung at his neck. It took several chops to sever the head. Great swaths of blood drenched his arms and chest and face by then.

Such creatures ought not to be allowed to rise as draugar. He didn't think a man could rise without a head, but better to be certain. He tossed the head on top of the flaming house. Then he dragged the corpse over to the blaze.

"What have you done?" someone demanded. "You'll burn the whole fucking town to ash!"

Slagfid ignored him. The townsfolk could stop the flames from spreading. And now one of the Niflung sorcerers was dead.

One down.

Eight more to fulfill his oath.

THE GRIMACE on her face meant Kelda struggled not to cry out as the völva held her arm by the hearth fire. Her frostbitten flesh had changed from blue to a pale, icy white, and she shivered like deathchill threatened her. Slagfid glowered. By the ghosts of his ancestors, he'd kill that Niflung again if he could. The princess deserved better than this, and the völva had spoken as though she might even lose the arm. Claimed she would *try* to save it.

"I've already slain a sorcerer this night," Slagfid had whispered in her ear. "Killing an old witch would be a small task beside that."

Of course, he would not harm the town völva, and she would know that. Nevertheless, her eyes had widened and she had not left the princess's side, though others bore similar injuries. The Niflung had killed men with his mere touch. Such powers did not bode well.

The Niflungar would learn Frothi's people had slain the emissary, and their assassins would return.

Finally, the völva pulled away from Kelda. "Remain by the fire and do not fall asleep. Keep the arm moving." The old woman looked to Slagfid, and he nodded. Yes, her task was done, and she could see to the others.

When she left, he knelt beside Kelda. She did not look at him. On long nights of patrol, she had demonstrated a keen enough mind and a sharper wit. They often boasted or traded good-natured insults with one another, and she'd won enough exchanges he'd challenged her to swordplay. That, he had won, causing her to storm off. Proud one this, but she deserved her pride. She was skilled, fast. Clever, even.

After a few moments she cleared her throat. "You saved my life. I admit it, all right? Now we are even."

"The thought had never crossed my mind. I promised I'd kill nine men for you, and I will fulfill that promise."

"Why?"

"I do not break my oaths."

"Oh? Hmm. And who is Svanhit?" She continued shifting her arm by the hearth.

Slagfid scowled at Kelda's back. He had not thought of his wife all day. Her ring no longer seemed warm. Besides, talking about her with Kelda felt wrong. No, she wouldn't understand. She had asked him this question on a few occasions before, and he avoided it.

"No one." The words tasted vile in his mouth. She was someone important. And he had made an oath to *her*, as well. He ran a thumb over the ring. Svanhit had made him laugh even more than Kelda had. He just needed to fulfill his oath to Kelda, then he'd find his wife. She'd understand —Hel, *she* had been the one to leave *him*. "Just get some rest."

Very soon, they would need every warrior they had.

16

AGILAZ

*W*inter had broken at last. Agilaz had spent the better part of it at Vestborg with Hermod and a few slaves granted to him by Hadding, as well as a handful of freemen he still trusted. Mostly trusted.

Now, with the storms no longer threatening, he could make the trek back to Halfhaugr without much worry. They had been on the road two days already and ought to reach the town by nightfall. Hermod walked beside him. He was growing strong, and Agilaz would not deny him any chance to learn of the World.

They had made no more raids during the winter. Agilaz was content he had stirred the Skalduns into a frenzy, though. Either they would retreat and return Hadding's lands, or else there would be outright war very soon. And if there was war, perhaps Olrun would finally show herself. He refused to give up hope. She was here, he could feel her still, through her glittering ring. Sometimes, he almost felt she watched him, even watched over him. Maybe his victories in the winter had come, in part, thanks to her grace. That was what he told Hermod, at least. It cheered the boy to learn his mother remained nigh, helping them.

When the boy held the ring, he'd said he also heard Olrun's song, sweet and forlorn. How did such a young boy even know a word like *forlorn*? And why had Agilaz never realized Olrun's songs held such undertones? They did; he could say that now. Maybe she'd always known she would be called back, that her respite was temporary. He would not believe that, though. He was going to find her and bring her home.

Once, returning to Halfhaugr had been a welcome event. Once, he had allowed himself to care, to forget this place was not home. Without Olrun, no home existed. Erik's betrayal had reminded him of that. Seeing that thick wooden wall brought him no pleasure now. Still, what would Hadding do with his summer? Hide behind these walls again? Or take the battle to the Skalduns at last? The latter, with any luck.

Patience was wisdom. And still, Agilaz's patience had worn thin through the dark, cold moons he'd spent at Vestborg, alone without his wife.

The men and women of the court welcomed him back as though naught had gone wrong a few moons before. They greeted Hermod and asked over how the winter had gone out west. His son replied politely, while Agilaz made his way toward Hadding.

Liv caught his eye before he reached the jarl. Her belly was swollen, far along. Erik's unborn son or daughter? And would she tell the child how Agilaz had slain its father? A man he called friend, burned to death by his hand. Liv ducked away before he could speak to her. So be it. What could he say, in any event? Maybe she had misconstrued his intentions toward her, or maybe only her husband had.

Either way, he could not change it now, much as he wished to. It haunted him at night.

Betrayal. The smell of flesh burning. Screams.

Agilaz shook himself. He had not come here to dwell on such deeds.

Many of the men in the hall seemed outfitted for war, freshly so. A good sign.

Jarl Hadding sat at his table, feasting a new guest. A blond-haired young man just past twenty winters, Agilaz would guess.

The jarl waved at him as he approached.

"Ah, come, Agilaz. You've not met Prince Otwin."

"Prince?" The Aesir had not had a king in generations. No two tribes could remain allied long enough.

The young man rose. "I am the eldest son of King Nidud of Njarar." He spoke with a pomposity that made Agilaz instantly hate him.

He had heard the name before. Nidud was one of the seven kings in Sviarland. "You are far from home, prince."

"So speaks the Kvenlander," Hadding said. "Prince Otwin brings us an offer of alliance, of trade. Have you seen the armor they bring to us? So fine you'd think dvergar themselves crafted it."

"Oh?" Agilaz took a longer look at the mail Otwin wore. It was fine work, as far as he could tell, though he was no expert on such things. But if Hadding was … "Dvergar, you say?"

Had the dvergar actually left Nidavellir? Or did they just have some trade agreement with Nidud? Either way, every step they drew closer to this place was an unwelcome one.

"Not actually," Otwin said. "My father has employed a great smith trained by them, though. His works are unmatched in all the North Realms." The boy patted a sword hanging over his shoulder. "He made this as well. It is remarkable."

Agilaz frowned, but nodded. There was only one smith trained by dvergar, and Agilaz did not think Volund like to seek employment with some petty king. Maybe he was wrong. Maybe his brother had done as Agilaz himself had done with Hadding. And yet, if he were crafting so many things to outfit the Hasdingi for war ... why? Why would Volund do it, and why would Nidud want him to outfit the Hasdingi? What would a Sviarland king profit from war among the Ás tribes?

"Sit, Agilaz, sit," Hadding commanded. "Someone get the man some mead. Frey! I will not have it said I am a poor host."

Agilaz did sink down onto the bench and lose himself in drink. It gave him time to mull over this development. Maybe Nidud wanted the Hasdingi to win a war so he'd have favorable trade partners in Aujum. Or maybe he wanted an Ás tribe in his debt. If he armed them with finer weapons and armor than their foes—as aught made by Volund would be—then surely the Hasdingi would win the war.

But what of Volund? He had once claimed that working those forges was his greatest love and his greatest fear, both. That it brought something out of him, something dark he did not wish to face. If there was a chance Nidud was forcing him to it, Agilaz had to find out. He owed his brother that much.

❧

AFTER THE FEASTING HAD SLOWED, and warriors had begun to drift away from Hadding's mead bench, Agilaz stood up.

He had not wanted to be the first to leave. He nodded to Otwin and the jarl and left.

He found Hermod outside Frigg's room. He motioned with his head down the hall. Hermod left Frigg's game and followed his father.

"You need to prepare for another journey," Agilaz said.

Hermod opened his mouth as if to protest, but closed it quickly. "Where are we going?" he asked after a moment.

"North. We are going to your Uncle Volund."

17

VOLUND

*V*olund tossed the helm onto the pile of other workings for the moon. A mail shirt, arrowheads, a golden brooch. The knife, that too. The keenest of edges on that one. Once a moon, the king's men would come, claim his works. Oh, and praise him as the greatest smith in Midgard. Nidud honored his word in that.

And they brought him any material he desired. He had but to ask and they delivered ivory, gems, obsidian. Aught he could use in his designs.

With a sigh, Volund limped over to the table where he worked on a ring from time to time. From memory he'd tried to craft another duplicate of Altvir's ring. They had taken all those he had once made. In truth, he cared little about the gold and silver stolen. One more crime, and one for which he needed to add but a small measure more to his planned vengeance. But the orichalcum ring of the valkyrie, that he needed. He no longer saw her. No, even in dreams she was far off, out of his reach. Ever fleeing into darkness. Or fleeing from the darkness that had so enveloped him.

That thought made him chuckle. He lurked down here in the forge like a wraith haunting some ancient barrow.

Grunting, he leaned on the table and held the ring up to his face. Useless. Why could he not remember the exact look, the proportions? Maybe it was a vain hope that Altvir's ring could still save him. Even had the bitch queen not given it to her daughter—a girl Volund had never even seen—there was no telling if it could save him. He would never walk again, not as a man. As his dvergar masters hobbled around in pain, so too had he become a twisted shell.

His right leg had become useless. In truth, he had almost died under the ministrations of Nidud's half-competent völva. He wanted to call it luck that he had not bled to death. But somehow, Volund doubted luck had much to do with it. Perhaps it was his cursed urd, placed upon him by a cackling Norn. Or perhaps it was whatever the dvergar had done to him in the deeps of Nidavellir.

For they had done something.

He caught a glimpse of his reflection in the still lake. His skin had become ashen, as if so many moons in the shadows had sapped the color from him, save for his hair. That had, when he tried washing it in the lake, shone like onyx.

Either way, had he bled to death, it might have been a mercy compared to this wretched existence. The forge itself was his sole solace, at least as long as he tried to forget he crafted these treasures for the very man who maimed him.

Sapphire shrooms grew around the forge, and the oblivion they offered had eased him through the agonies of his injury. He no longer needed them, but still, sometimes he imbibed them. The shadows danced for him when he did.

Volund sighed. There was no point to finishing the ring. Let Nidud take it and trade it to pay for his wars. Perhaps it did not duplicate Altvir's treasure—still it was finer than aught most men would ever lay eyes on.

He is coming.

Volund jerked his head up. They came once a day, as best he could tell, to bring him food. Only a few hours had passed since the last visit. And it didn't seem time for anyone to claim the treasures. So then who?

No. He didn't care. He no longer went out to meet them when they came. Thakkrad had ordered the bridge extended just enough a man could leap from it to the island. A man with both legs at least. It was his little torture, dangling freedom so close but ever out of reach. Volund had crafted a cane, hobbled out to meet them many times. But it did not take long to tire of their mockery. So instead, he remained in the forge. Let them leave his food and go.

Here, between flame and shadow, he worked, ate, and slept. And he dreamed, ever chasing Altvir through the dark. Perhaps it was him she fled.

He is here.

Volund grumbled, then grabbed his cane before hobbling over to the forge entrance. One of Nidud's sons stood there. Perhaps nineteen, twenty winters. Not so very many less than Volund himself. The man wore mail—armor Volund himself had crafted a few moons back—but no guards accompanied him. The strange smith who had once frightened an entire court was now a mockery, feared by none in his lameness. More fools them.

The young man looked around the forge, working his jaw in obvious unease. Perhaps that ought to be a small comfort to Volund. If the whelp didn't fear him, at least he seemed uncomfortable.

"What do you want here, boy?"

Instead of answering, he knelt to inspect the pile of goods Volund was working on.

"Like what you see, boy?"

"My name is Ulf Nidudson, and I am no boy." He rose, turning on Volund with all the false bravado Amelias had once shown.

Volund watched him, unmoving.

"How did you make Mimung?" Ulf asked after a moment.

So that was what this boy intended. Interesting. Volund had explained to both Thakkrad and Nidud directly that he could forge no more runeblades. There was no more orichalcum, a fact that the king, at least, had finally been persuaded to believe. Nidud had given Mimung to his eldest son, Otwin, the one fighting battles with the Aesir. That made Ulf, the middle brother, left behind. Inheriting naught but second place and maybe a chance to serve as his brother's shadow. Not unlike the urd Agilaz might have found beneath Slagfid, had any of them ever returned to Kvenland.

Strange, he had not thought of his half-brothers in some time.

Oh, well. Here he was, face to face with one of the sons of Nidud. And the king must not know he was here. Because Nidud already knew Volund had used the last of the orichalcum to forge Mimung.

Volund nodded at him. "Eager to step out of your brother's shadow, are you? Maybe with such a sword you could go off to war, too. Find glory." Volund flicked some soot off his nails. "And if dear Otwin were to fall in battle, well ..."

The boy glowered and stalked closer. "My brother is not the only one who stands in the way."

Oh. Oh, that was rich. "You will use a sword I make to kill your father?"

Ulf shook his head. "You know what kind of king he is. He's lived too long and now he's like to ruin our whole kingdom with his wars. We have the wealth to prosper, but he will not be content until he owns everything between here and the Midgard Wall."

A well-practiced speech. And probably at least half-true. Nidud's ambition would lead to his downfall, maybe sooner than even Ulf seemed to realize.

"And if I made such a work for you, in secret ... what reward might I expect?"

Ulf shrugged. "Your freedom."

At that, Volund did laugh. "You would let me go? *Where*? How? Should I walk down the mountain? Men had to carry me down those steps leading up to the hall. I would not make it on my own, not even to that town. Your father has ruined me."

"Then take revenge."

Oh, he would. Nidud had once promised him suffering even skalds would hesitate to speak of. That was what Volund intended to deliver to him. One day.

Until then ...

"How old is your sister?"

Ulf spread his hands. "Bodvild? Uh, sixteen winters."

"Married?"

"No. Father's been saving her for a worthy bride price, or so he says. She's mother's favorite, and the queen will not be parted from her."

How perfect. "And pretty?"

"I don't fancy my own sister."

Volund smirked at that. The boy wasn't half so bad as his father. "Your father had me maimed and imprisoned without knowing who I was. He never stopped to ask. My father was a prince of Kvenland. A bastard prince, but a prince nonetheless. I stand to inherit no throne, but I am an eligible man, one of a worthy line."

Ulf grinned. "And you want to marry my sister. Well, that's perfect, of course. You can't make it on your own ... but instead of being a prisoner here, you could be the most honored man in the court. The royal armorer, husband to the princess."

The boy was clever. After a fashion. Volund didn't much care whether Bodvild was pretty, and he was already married. But the princess had Altvir's ring, and if she was the queen's favorite, maybe he would kill her just to punish the mother.

"So start forging the blade."

"I will see the girl first."

"I cannot give you her hand while my father yet lives."

"Then arrange a meeting, and I ..."

Someone watches. Someone listens. Someone learns.

Volund tried to keep his expression the same. Had Ulf brought a guard? No, someone had come after the prince.

He hobbled over to the treasure pile. Once there, he almost fell as he knelt down to examine it. He steadied himself on the helmet, while grabbing the knife.

"Arrange a meeting with the girl. For now, you can take this helm. It's stronger than most and will keep you safe, should you join your brother in war."

Ulf took the helm and tried it on. Volund hobbled around the forge, cane thumping with every step.

Now that he knew, he could hardly see how he'd missed the other boy, hiding in the shadows. He could *feel* the child and his beating heart, disrupting the darkness. And from the corner of his eye, he could see him. Nidud's younger son. Short blond hair like his older brother, a leather jerkin.

Hand clutching a sword, thinking himself unseen. Fifteen winters, maybe.

"Ulf?" Volund said.

The man, now helmed, approached.

"I take it your father does not know you've come here?"

"Of course he doesn't fucking know. You take me for a fool?"

"And did you invite your brother to join us?"

"What?"

Volund pointed his cane at the boy lurking in the shadows.

Ulf took a few steps in that direction, then started. "Snorre!"

That complicated things. If they had been working together it would be bad enough—two tongues that might wag. But to have the one spying on the other ... What a family.

The younger stepped from the shadows, shaking his head as if unable to fathom how Volund knew of his presence. "Father will have you strung from the platform for this one, Ulf. I hear if you hang there long enough, your balls literally freeze off."

Volund approached behind Ulf. "He's going to ruin your plan."

"Snorre, you will say naught of this to Father or anyone else."

The urge to roll his eyes was almost overwhelming. "Yes, that will work. Threaten him, too, perhaps. No one knows he came here. Just kill him."

Ulf spun on him. "Kill my brother?"

"You were willing to kill your *other* brother." And his father.

Snorre spat. "He wouldn't dare try! I'll cut your legs as bad as that smith's!"

Ulf hesitated, hand on his sword hilt but not drawing it. Useless. The man lacked the conviction to see things through. Nor was his plan sure to result in Nidud receiving his full measure of suffering.

Shame, though. It had been tempting.

Volund slipped his knife between Ulf's ribs. The blade pierced the mail and the man's heart. Ulf slumped forward, trying to turn, as if to ask why. Snorre stood there, mouth agape. Volund flung his cane end-over-end into the younger boy's face. It landed with a sick crack, and the boy fell into a heap, gasping.

Now the hard part. Volund jerked his knife free and limped slowly to Snorre. He knelt beside the boy—who, to his credit, tried to grab that sword. With a swift jerk Volund cut his throat.

Hot blood exploded outward and washed over Volund's face. No different than slaughtering a deer, after all.

Volund groaned as he rose. Well, perhaps he was going to get a measure of vengeance today. The king would wonder where his sons had gone, of course. Whatever lived in the lake would take care of the bodies. But before that, well, Durin had shown him how to make a stunning goblet from a man's skull. Perhaps that would impress Nidud, at least while he thought it walrus ivory or some such.

And then he ought to make something for the queen. Teeth could be shaved into some exquisite ivory brooches.

Yes, the royal couple would be so happy today.

18

DAYS GONE

Nine Years Ago

*A*gilaz had been the one to point out the dvergar would expect Volund to return east to Kvenland. That had left them only one remaining choice—to travel south, into the kingdoms of Sviarland. And still, they could not risk any of the nearer lands reporting on their passage. Thus, the brothers had stuck to the woods, the wilds, hunting, foraging. Two moons had come and gone before the first time they allowed themselves to trade in a town, and even then, Agilaz went alone.

But now the days grew shorter, summer waning. Soon, the winter storms would begin, and they could not hope to weather six moons as they were, in the wilds, without proper shelter. They had discussed hunting for caves, but Agilaz insisted they might spend far too long seeking one suitable.

The mist was thick down here, in the valleys. Thick enough the light didn't bother his eyes as it had when he first emerged from Nidavellir.

Volund pitched another stone into the river, watching the splash. It would freeze soon. Just like them. "You two ought to return to Kvenland." It was not the first time he had suggested it. The dvergar would hunt him for the rest of his days, but, with any luck, they didn't know his brothers had even been there. Why, then, should Agilaz and Slagfid give up everything and suffer?

Sometimes, he imagined the sunlight had touched Durin, had truly turned the dverg to stone as in legends. It was an idle fancy, and would only make Dvalin's vengeance upon him more dire.

Slagfid scoffed. "Who do you imagine will wish to ferry us across the Gandvik this time of year? Most captains find the sudden storms a bit inconvenient, what with the capsizing and horrible deaths at sea." His eldest brother was whittling down an arrow for Agilaz, something to hunt for the night meal. Volund did not chide his brother, though he could have done better himself. His heart was not in the crafting, and Slagfid did not push him much. "Or maybe you meant we should travel back north through Nidavellir the way we just came?"

Agilaz frowned as if Slagfid's suggestion was in earnest. "Too dangerous. Besides, even if we returned to Kvenland, grandfather would not risk arousing the ire of Nidavellir to shelter the sons of his bastard."

Volund flung another stone into the river. Because of his actions, his brothers had lost their home as well. He could have stayed, given himself over to service to the dvergar.

No. He would not be owned, not by them, not by anyone.

Agilaz grabbed his arm. "Be still. Do not disturb any vaettir slumbering in the river."

Volund scowled, not denying the reprimand. Yes, he should have known better. Wild rivers were oft home to nixies or other spirits apt to drag a man to his death. Part of him almost welcomed such a challenge, a chance to vent his ever-growing frustration, his anger, on aught, whether deserving or not.

His middle brother pointed to the south. "This river runs to the heart of the valley, feeds a lake there. The townsfolk do not go there."

"Why not?" Volund asked. Sviarland was covered in lakes, many of which proved ideal locations for towns, trade stops, or small farms.

In answer, Agilaz moved along the riverbank and knelt beside it. What was he on about now? Volund stalked closer to inspect whatever had drawn his brother's attention. A wolf's paw print, deep in the mud around the river. Very deep and very large. "Dire wolves. They hunt this whole valley."

Slagfid snorted. "Then maybe you ought not to have led us here, little brother. I for one think there might be easier game than any wolf, much less dire wolves."

Volund found he had to agree. Such animals roamed the wilds in Kvenland, and while they were not much larger than gray wolves, they were heavier and had much stronger teeth. More importantly, they would prey on Mankind, while a gray wolf would only do so if starving or cornered. "What are you thinking, brother?"

"I'm thinking Agilaz is drunk," Slagfid said.

"I was not talking to you."

Agilaz scowled at Slagfid. "No one will come looking for us in this valley. Men avoid it, which means though some king might claim the land in practice, none will stop us from taking it for ourselves."

"Right," Slagfid save. "Except maybe the *fucking* dire wolves."

Agilaz shrugged. "We have bows. You risked your life against the dvergar, but you will run from animals? This may prove our best chance."

Volund rose. "I say we find the lake." The wolf print was deep, yes. And wolves of any sort were territorial. If the brothers wanted to claim a place here, they'd probably have to fight for it. But Agilaz was right—it was better than risking word getting back to Nidavellir. Here, they might have peace.

Slagfid held up his hand. "I am the oldest, it ought to be my decision."

"And?" Volund asked.

Slagfid rubbed his beard. "Well ... I've decided we should go to the lake."

Volund cast a glance at Agilaz. His middle brother nodded sternly. Volund sighed.

IN HIS DREAMS, a world of shadows danced and played, its laughter a muted cacophony of madness. It called to him, whispering of pleasures found in the places where no light had ever reached, taunting him of the weakness inherent in the world he clung to still.

And so, Volund did not sleep too often. He sat through the ever-lengthening nights with his back to the fire, staring off into the woods. The wolves were out there, howling, stalking. Their anger saturated the air. No, they did not like that Men had dared settle in their valley, had begun cutting timber to build their house. The foundations of it were set already, the fire pit dug and set ablaze. That kept the beasts at bay. That and, perhaps, that Agilaz had put an arrow through the eye of one who had drawn too close.

Volund's brother slept on a wolf pelt now. Soundly, as did Slagfid. Volund had told them he would watch through the night. If sleep was to be denied him, why should he not at least allow his brothers respite? And what did they dream of? Girls, perhaps.

It had been too long now since Volund had had a slave girl. The dvergar had given him the habit of spending himself before sleep. And those dreams, when he found them, they showed him flickers of flesh in the darkness. Daring him, demanding he hunt down some farm girl and ravish her. Even now, awake, it was like having a serpent constricting his gut. Squeezing him, pushing him toward his insatiable need.

He gagged on it and stumbled away from the fire. A glance in that direction nigh blinded him. It was so bright. Volund scrambled away from the flames, stumbled his way to the lake, and fell to his knees there. Beneath the surface, flesh writhed in a mass of tits and arses and trenches begging to be plowed.

"No," he sobbed. "Stop it. Get out of my head."

He plunged his face into the water. Its icy chill beat the salacious thoughts away. There was peace down in the murk. If he but held his head under a few moments longer, all suffering would abate forever. Just hold it there and let oblivion take him, sweep him down into the frozen under-world of Hel, where twisted souls such as his own must surely belong.

His lungs burned. His arms twitched.

Of its own volition, his head jerked upward into the air, and he sucked down great lungfuls of it in painful gasps. Unable to catch his breath, he pitched over backward and lay in the wet mud. The mist was thick over the lake, and here he was, breathing it deeply. Welcoming Mist-madness.

The men of Kvenland claimed that mist would steal souls and memories. According to the dvergar, the latter was true. Memories faded, replaced with a corrupted poison of Niflheim. What would such poison do to a Man, were he to accept it willingly? Should one welcome the fading of memories, would it then become a painless transition into whatever haunted state the mist would leave in place of a Man? No. That seemed unlikely. There was no end to pain in this World. That lesson the dvergar had taught him with clarity, their cruelty merely a reflection of their own unending agony.

Such was the way of the World.

And they had put it in him. That cruelty, that wicked perception that had no place beneath the sunlight. As indeed, the light still felt too hot upon his skin, on rare mornings when the mist was too thin. He, like some accursed vaettr, now felt shelter in that poisoned mist. Hel damn Dvalin and all his people and Volund's own father for sending him to the dvergar. They had done something to him. Gods above, had he but left when his first year was ended, he might have escaped this.

What if they had ... had put one of their own—

The lake exploded upward like a geyser.

Volund jerked to a sitting position as the waters showered him. It was like a jotunn had tossed a rock into the lake, but no such monster ought to be here, on the wrong side of the Midgard Wall. He reached for his sword. Damn. Still resting by the fire.

Something splashed around out in the water.

"Who's there?"

A cry of pain. A woman's voice.

Volund stared dumbly at the waters. Some nixie trick perhaps, a ploy to lure him into the river where she could drown him. If so, then he welcomed such a reprieve. Volund waded into the waters, waist deep. Freezing, so cold he already could not feel his legs as he stumbled around.

But he could see. Despite the mist blocking all starlight, he saw the woman, splashing around, trying to pull herself to the surface. Volund grabbed her, throwing her arm around his shoulders. She struggled—stronger than a woman ought to be. Volund pulled her ashore and dropped her in the mud.

Her soaked blonde hair spread out wildly. Her gown was torn, soaked in blood. Volund knelt beside her and pulled it away, revealing the glint of golden armor beneath it. Blood caked that too, seeping from a gap between plates over her ribs. The workmanship was Otherworldly: even a glance revealed that much. Not dverg make, though, and he knew little of the crafts of other vaettir. The liosalfar favored golden armor, he supposed. Could she be an alf? She was glorious indeed.

The armor was held on by latches, which he began to pop one by one. She groaned, swatting at him. Despite her eyes being closed, she was still strong. Inhumanly so. Had she been more than half conscious, he probably couldn't have managed this. With a third clasp open, he pulled the plate away, exposing her ribs. A severe wound had pierced her side. Not an arrow—it was too big. Someone had thrust a spear through her. The question was how? A man might have slipped a knife between those plates, but not a spear.

He pushed away her undershirt to better examine the wound. In doing so, he exposed one of her breasts. And could not stop from reaching for it. All her muscles were toned as a warrior, but her breast was still soft. As would be her … He looked to her legs. To where the trench between them would be if he but pulled away that cloth. So thin a piece of fabric keeping him from even a moment of reprieve from the pain, from the darkness *they* had planted in him. It was growing, he could feel it. If he just buried himself inside this woman he could be spared for a night, at least.

Oh, fuck. Gods above and Hel below. He jerked a dagger loose from his belt. His hand shook. Slowly, he drew the blade along his arm, trying to relish the pain. It was a welcome distraction from his unsavory lust. No matter what the dvergar had done to him, he was not going to rape this woman. They had subjected him to that on several occasions—as much to break him as out of any desire to do so, he suspected. He would not become one of them. No, not if he could help it. Though, had they planted one of their nascent souls inside him, perhaps that was how he changed. Was he losing himself to possession by a dverg soul?

He looked back at the blonde woman, bleeding out in the mud. A dverg would have plowed her trench and then thrown her back in the water. That was not what Volund would do. He was still a Man.

After lifting the woman in his arms, he carried her back to the house's foundations. "Brothers!"

SHE SHOULD HAVE DIED. A mortal woman would have perished from any such injury. Instead, the woman—or alf, if she was—clung to life. Her color returned not long after Agilaz had bound her wounds. She stirred in restless fits, though, turning, twisting, and crying out as though engaged in a pitched battle. Perhaps she was, albeit a battle not to be won with spear or sword.

Agilaz and Slagfid sat aside, arguing over the woman and who she might be. They wondered if she was Sviarlander, or a barbarian Ás shieldmaiden, or some wanderer. The latter seemed most likely, though Volund said naught. The thought of explaining to his brothers he suspected this was no human at all tasted foul on his tongue. What strange twisting of urd had caused this woman to plummet into their sheltered valley?

Not quite certain why, he leaned forward and held the woman's hand. It was hot, clammy, perhaps even feverish. She should have died, but she hadn't. She shouldn't have been here at all. But she was. And while he clasped her hand, while he watched her struggling face, no longer did he feel compelled to give in to violence or darkness. All he could think was how to save her. As if Freyja or some other Vanr had heard his prayers and offered him a purpose to his twisted existence.

A cold metal band touched his fingers. She wore a ring. He pulled her hand closer to examine it. The most intricate of designs decorated it. Swan feathers, perhaps, etched into orichalcum.

Not sure why he did it, Volund pressed the ring to his lips and kissed her knuckles.

WITH DAWN, the brothers resumed cutting timber. Volund stopped every so often to check on the woman, who remained by the fire, soaking in its warmth.

The air had grown chill. Snow would fall very soon, and they needed to have the walls built, or dire wolves would feast on their frozen corpses. His brothers deferred to his orders, trusting he knew best how to construct a hall. He did, of course. He had learned architecture from the finest architects on Midgard, after all. He could not quite decide whether he hated the dvergar. They had tortured him, perhaps even implanted something in his soul, something slowly taking him over. And yet, they had taught him secrets and wisdom no man had ever known.

Once, Dvalin had spoken of Midgard as it was in another Era of the World. An Era before the coming of the mists, when Mankind ruled the land and they, too, had known and built wonders. Perhaps the dverg spoke of such times as one more torment, meant to shame him with the knowledge of all his people had lost. Somehow, though, it made Volund dare to dream he might help Mankind return to those days.

As soon as the house was done, he'd start on the wall. They'd want a strong one to keep the wolves at bay, just in case the fire was not enough.

Of a sudden, Agilaz dropped the plank he carried and turned to the south. A pair of women stood there, golden armor glittering in the sunlight. More impressive still, they each bore great wings spread out behind them. Both women were blonde like the one within, somewhat similar of feature. One had brown wings, the other silver.

Slagfid, too, had come to stare openmouthed at them.

At the valkyries.

The dvergar had not spoken of such things, and Volund had thought them mere legends. Choosers of the slain who came to take the greatest warriors to some blessed afterlife. They claimed the souls of great warriors. Like the woman he had saved.

Volund tossed his tools aside and drew his sword, advancing on the valkyrie pair. "If you've come for her soul, you shall pay dearly for it."

The silver-winged valkyrie scowled and drew a sword, while the other laughed.

The laughing one strode forward. Her hand rested on a sword at her hip, but she did not draw it. "You are a bold one, to think to defend anyone from us."

"Damn it, little brother," Slagfid mumbled. "What are you getting us into this time?"

Agilaz edged his way toward the house. His bow was there, but he'd never make it. Volund tried to wave him to stillness, lest the valkyries attack.

"Do not come between us and Altvir," the other valkyrie said. She advanced a few steps, spear ready.

It was madness to stand before valkyries. Had they come to claim this Altvir's soul, it surely meant she was already dying, despite his best efforts. Moreover, fighting valkyries was apt to get his own brothers killed.

Somehow, Volund still could not sheath his sword. "You will not have her while there is life left in her."

The silver-winged valkyrie leapt into the air. Her wings flung her upward which such force the wind of it swept Volund from his feet. He crashed to the ground, the impact stinging. Somehow, he managed to hold onto his sword. The valkyrie landed astride him and hefted him upward by his tunic with one hand. The other hand held her sword a hairsbreadth from his eye. Her own eyes were pale blue, but they seemed to blaze with Otherworldly fire, demanding he not look away. Holding him bound to her power.

And then it hit him. This valkyrie was stronger than any woman, blessed with supernatural grace and power. "Altvir is one of you."

"Yes. I am." The voice came from behind them. It was weak, a little raspy. "Release him, Olrun. He's only tried to help me."

Volund felt ill. Here she was, defending him after he had almost ...

The silver-winged one—Olrun—dropped him, and he landed on his feet. "They do not hold you against your will?"

Altvir looked down at her bandaged side, then pointedly at Volund. "I think he fished me out of the lake."

Olrun scowled, but the other valkyrie walked forward with a half-smile. As she did so, the wings receded into her back, vanishing. Olrun planted her sword in the ground and folded her arms, but made no move to retract those beautiful silver wings of hers.

"Will you live?" Volund asked Altvir.

She smiled and held up her hand, displaying the ring. Did that grant her the powers she wielded? "I will, thanks to you. Most wounds heal. Drowning does not."

Agilaz had continued to move toward the house and now snatched up a torch from the fire pit, holding it before himself in warding. Volund chuckled. Fire kept Mist spirits at bay, and others—Dark spirits, Water spirits, were none too fond of it. It was not like to hold much fear for these valkyries, though. He did not know their true nature, but they clearly did not fear to walk in daylight. Which meant if they were vaettir at all, they did not hail from Niflheim or Svartalfheim.

All three valkyries looked at him, then glanced at Volund. Altvir walked forward slowly, the effort an obvious pain to her. Volund closed the distance between them in a few strides.

The brown-winged valkyrie had begun to walk toward the lake. Volund glanced at her, then focused on Altvir. "What is it, my lady?"

Altvir placed a hand on his shoulder, seeming to support herself that way. In fact, she seemed ready to pitch forward at any moment. "A man who aids a valkyrie is entitled any wish in her power to grant."

"Ask her for a night," Slagfid said.

Volund struggled to keep his face emotionless. The very thought had crossed his mind, though perhaps not for the reason Slagfid thought. Men told stories about the valkyries. They lusted after them even as they feared them, and it was said if one could win such an embrace and please a valkyrie, one would inherit glory and an almost fey insight. And he wanted her so badly it hurt. Not just in his cock and aching balls, but in his gut. In the hollow of his chest. It was more than all that, though. Altvir's green eyes were somehow luminous, like the sun. But unlike the sun, he could look into them and feel no pain, no burn. Feel no desire to return to the shadows.

"Marry me." The words escaped him almost unbidden.

Her mouth opened, eyes wide. She might well strike him down for such temerity. If that was her wish, he found the thought acceptable. Just to touch the light, if only for a moment.

"I have an oath to keep," Altvir said, her voice trembling a little. "I am a chooser of the slain."

"Make a new oath. An oath to me. And I will be only yours. Is that not in your power to grant?"

"Altvir ..." Olrun's voice had a hint of warning, and yet, almost an edge of longing. Part of her approved, wanted it for her sister. Volund knew she did.

"You hesitate, then," Volund said. In the end, the bold might find early graves. But they alone took all the glory and all that was worth having in life, while those who cowered in fear languished in envy. Such was the way of the World. "I will change my wish. Three valkyries. Three brothers. You each marry one of us."

Olrun's wings stirred the air. "I ought to eviscerate you for such arrogance."

"Be that as it may, I did save Altvir. And that is my wish. I leave it to you whether to grant it."

"I do not speak for my sisters," Altvir said. She looked at Olrun, then at the other, who now returned from the lake bearing a sword. Altvir's? It must have fallen when she did. "Their choice is their own, and they are not bound by custom to honor your wishes. I, for one, though ... I will stay with you. As much as I am able."

Volund flung his arms around her and kissed her, then. Altvir returned his embrace, stiffly at first, then without reservation. Unbidden, a tear crept from the corner of his eye.

꙳

VOLUND WEPT AGAIN as he spent himself in her. He had felt many women climax beneath him. This was different. A wave of light crashed into him and scoured him from the inside out, suffusing his soul and silencing the wicked shadows that thought to command him.

Peace and warmth surrounded him as much as her arms and legs did. Whatever the dvergar had tried to plant in him, Altvir killed it, burned it away in her light.

Her eyes looked so deeply into his he could see the glory of all the World.

Of his salvation.

To his surprise, the other two had agreed to marry his brothers. Perhaps they did so to remain with Altvir, or perhaps they too longed for a simple life, removed from the death they must witness without end. Or maybe he would never understand their reasons.

Olrun, who spoke little, chose Agilaz. Volund supposed their natures were similar enough. They seemed keen to walk the woods alone together, hunting, snaring. It was hard to imagine there being much conversation, but then, perhaps they spoke without words.

And Slagfid had seemed more than happy with the last valkyrie—Svanhit. Volund's eldest brother was probably happy to bed any valkyrie, and twice thrilled to spend his life with one who seemed to appreciate his sense of humor. And Svanhit's laughter did often grace the night.

His brothers had slept with their new wives as soon as they were wed, he had no doubt. Altvir—despite his desires—he had insisted recover more fully before they lay together. Tonight she had come to him and told him it was time. Three days since they'd wed and they had finally consummated it.

He lay stroking her hair for a time.

And when he slept, he dreamt of sunlight dancing over green fields and lush forests where shadows fled his presence.

19

SLAGFID

A lingering silence had spread over Frothi's kingdom in the wake of the Niflung's death. Men called Slagfid a hero, and women offered themselves to him in drunken frenzies, their anger over the burnt house drowned in the flush of a sole victory. He turned them away—most of them. He did not feel a hero. He felt a man staring into the calm before the worst of winter storms, knowing it was coming.

And it did.

It took some time before they heard of it, though. An entire town swept away in a night of blood and torment, the dead left to rot upon spears stuck in the ground. The lucky ones. Some few warriors had risen as draugar, now plaguing the night, preying on those who dared chance the wilds.

Terror kept men from farming or fishing. Everywhere, the mist spread and shadows deepened. Men spoke now of compliance, of pledging eternal fealty, even. They spoke of all Reidgotaland serving the Niflungar, of the return of the Old Kingdoms.

Both of Frothi's jarls now lay murdered in their own homes. The assassin had slipped past their men and gutted them, then vanished into the night. Perhaps Frothi would have bent his knee, had Kelda not demanded otherwise.

Now Slagfid's party pushed on to the mountain peaks overlooking the town, though it had meant a night in the wilds. Nine men and women in their party, and not one had slept. All had gathered in a ring, close around the fire as they could. Slagfid had insisted they set up a ring of torches surrounding the camp. Morning, long in coming, had arrived and allowed them to continue up the mountain. Already, the day had drawn on.

The next Niflung assassin hunted them—he could feel it. There was a thickness to the mist, a foulness beyond even the norm. And ravens seemed to watch their every move, as if waiting for a new corpse to feast upon.

"Have you ever met this witch?" Slagfid asked.

Kelda grunted. The path had grown so steep, they had to use their hands to grab rocks and aid the ascent. "My father climbed this way, just before he became king. She does not like visitors."

"Imagine that." The town völva had told them to seek out her mentor, that she might have some wisdom with which to arm themselves. Given that the old woman could have been a grandmother, this other völva must have been ancient. And since she kept to herself atop the damn mountain, very few petitioners disturbed her rest.

Today they had climbed high enough even the mist lay below them, choking the land like a blanket of poison. The pure, unfiltered sunlight stung his eyes and lit the glorious sky. Sadly, though, it would not last but a few more hours.

They climbed on until his legs ached from it, until his

palms were worn raw. How some old woman made this ascent he would never guess. By the ghosts of his ancestors, this völva better have something real for them to use. They had risked their lives, made this climb, and left the town without its best protectors. All to get advice from an old woman who might have heard the voices of the gods ... or might have just been Mist-mad.

He'd been weaned on the tales—horrific some of them —of the Witch-Queens of Pohjola, and the admonition never to meddle in the affairs of such women. For his part, Slagfid took the völvur here as much the same as the witches of Kvenland. Best left alone.

But Kelda insisted. She believed in the völvur and their mysticism, a faith Slagfid almost envied in her.

At last they crested onto a plateau. The snows here had not melted. From the edge he stared down. You couldn't even see the damned ground through all that mist. If he did not know better, he might have sworn the mountain descended on forever, straight into Niflheim itself.

Kelda moved to stand beside him, while some of the others praised or implored the Vanir. Most had probably never seen such a view. "We're dying," Kelda said after a while.

"We'll find a way to kill this assassin. And seven more of his brothers."

"Maybe. But skalds talk about the Old Kingdoms, about how they once ruled the known world. And what are we now? Tiny tribes and kingdoms. And we kill each other over the few bits of land where food could grow."

Slagfid sighed. "There are great empires in the south, Miklagard and Serkland even beyond that."

"The only great kingdoms I know are those of fell

lineage," Kelda said, "peoples like the dvergar or the Niflungar. And a Niflung hunts us like frightened rabbits. I think all Mankind is dying out, or at least bound for slavery. We like to call Midgard our world, but it's not. Forget whatever horrors lay beyond the Midgard Wall. We are losing the World to the terrors on this side."

Slagfid grabbed her by the shoulders and spun her around. "You sound as morbid as my brother, and it suits you even less."

The princess shook her head then snorted. "Which brother?"

That got a laugh. "Volund, gods. Agilaz may have had his arsehole permanently frozen shut, but he's a practical one, grounded in the real world. Volund is the one given to such ..." He was going to say pointless, but it would have no doubt further darkened her mood. "... such dour musings."

"I find it hard not to be dour when faced with—"

"We are going to win. By the ghosts of my ancestors, Kelda, I'm going to give you eight more lives."

Kelda frowned a moment, staring out over the mist. Finally, she pointed to where the slope wound behind a bend. "I think this is it. The rest of you stay here. Slagfid and I will meet the völva alone."

He followed as she led. He had expected a hut atop the mountain, a tiny house maybe. Instead, they stood before a dome of rock, most of which was buried in snow. An open entrance lay in the middle, torch sconces burning on either side of it.

Slagfid glanced at Kelda, who shrugged. So—not what she was expecting either. Nice of Frothi to prepare them.

Naught else for it, though. They had come this far. After prying a torch loose, he entered the dome. Inside it was a hemisphere with a large fire pit in the center. Beyond the pit lay stairs descending into the mountain.

Someone groaned. Slagfid spun, sword in hand. Kelda forestalled him with a look that would have done Agilaz proud. Together, they advanced on the figure.

The crone wore a cloak, shrouding her face. When she reached a hand out, though, he could see why. Her skin was stretched so taut her bones seemed ready to pop right out of it, and numerous blemishes marred her misshapen hand. The fire's smoke did not quite cover the stench of old urine and rot that filled the dome.

"Ancient One," Kelda said, and knelt before the crone.

The woman's answer was a low moan. This witch was going to drop dead before she could reveal a damned thing. Still, he too knelt before her. They had come here for this. For *this*! Gods.

Desperation made fools of even wise men. And apparently of town völvur.

"Our kingdom is threatened."

"Mmmm."

Kelda glanced back at Slagfid. His turn to shrug. What did he know about such things?

The old woman reached into her cloak and pulled out a handful of bone tiles, each carved with a rune. She tossed them on the stone before her, then collapsed to the floor. Dead? No, she was leaning close, examining the runes.

She sat like that far too long. His knees hurt from the stone floor. The Mist-mad woman was wasting everyone's time. In fact, they needed to find a safe place to camp before nightfall. This errand might yet prove the death of them all.

With a groan, the völva sat back on her haunches. If that wasn't an invitation to do the same he wasn't like to get one.

The stone was cold on his arse, and more than aught he wanted to scoot closer to the fire pit.

The woman spoke. "You are hunted." Her throaty voice barely carried to where he sat a few feet away. "The Niflung assassin prince, Guthorm, stalks the island. Looks for you. Looks for ..." She pointed to the staircase descending into the mountain.

"He wants to enter the mountain?"

Kelda glared at him as if he had interrupted her. "Why? What is this place?"

"A Hilding burial chamber, the tomb of one of the great princes of old."

"Hildings?" Kelda asked.

This much, Slagfid did know. "One of the Old Kingdoms, enemies of the Niflungar. The Niflungar destroyed the kingdom and hunted down most of those claiming direct descent from Hildir. These people were quite possibly your ancestors, princess."

Her mouth hung open, though whether at the revelation itself, or the one delivering, he couldn't say. "Wh-what? I mean ... what do they want *here*? What good is a tomb from a dead kingdom?"

"That I don't ... No." He turned back to the völva. "*No*. Is it here? Is that what you mean, witch?"

"Mmmm." The crone nodded, her joints popping and creaking with the motion.

"Is what here?" Kelda demanded.

By the ghosts of his ancestors! As if things were not dire enough. And if this Guthorm tracked them up the mountain, they had led him right to it. He rose and started for the stairs, torch out before him. A thick layer of dust coated the steps and walls both, and the smell of rot grew stronger with each step down he took.

"Slagfid!" Kelda called after him. She followed. Not as though he had a right to keep her from this.

At the base of the stairs, a tunnel ran for a few fathoms before ending at a stone slab, sealing the tomb.

He sheathed his sword and handed Kelda the torch. He never should have made that oath to Njord. It had taken him so far from Svanhit ... and despite all the death, the valkyrie had not shown herself. Nor, in truth, had he given nigh as much thought to her in these past moons as in the first few.

"What is going on? I insist you tell me this instant."

Slagfid placed both hands against the slab and pushed. Dust spilled over him, stinging his eyes. Clogging his nostrils. He coughed, pulled away. Damn thing was heavy as a troll's arse.

"I might need your help here."

"First tell me what you expect to find."

"It's easier to show you, princess."

Grumbling, she set down the torch, then pressed her own hands on the slab. Together, they shoved. It creaked, stone grinding on stone, before finally giving way. It slid into a recess, revealing a circular tomb. A wave of stale air hit him, sent him into a coughing fit.

"Freya! What is that stench?"

Slagfid put the back of his hand to his face. "Old death." In the middle of the tomb lay a stone platform, upon which rested a skeleton.

In its hands, it clutched a sword, covered in a thick shroud of dust.

Somehow, he had almost hoped the crone was wrong, or lying. Not his urd, he supposed. Kelda pushed past him to stare at the corpse.

She looked like she planned to ask another question, so he strode up beside her. With his sleeve, he wiped the dust away from the sword. Doing so revealed beautifully etched runes running its length. The blade seemed to glitter in the torchlight.

"Behold, princess. The runeblade of the Hildings —Hrunting."

20

AGILAZ

*T*he Njarar king had his castle high up the mountain: a route that, even in summer, chilled Agilaz. Hermod made the climb without complaint, though his teeth chattered before they reached the main gate. Decent folk did not live in such places. Still, Agilaz had to admit any attack against this fortress was doomed. From the platform above, he alone could probably hold off a small army.

Despite the summer, ice still crusted the fortress, including the main gates. Guards with spears met him before he reached the landing, barring the way.

"I have come to see your king."

"And just who are you?"

"Agilaz, thegn of your ally, Jarl Hadding."

The guards exchanged glances, then one of them ordered a runner sent to the king. The men guarding the platform did not invite them up, so Agilaz wrapped an arm around his shivering son. So this was how King Nidud treated guests? It did not speak well for him, nor for Volund's likely urd here.

None of the men spoke.

Finally, the runner returned and whispered something in the ear of the guard who had sent him, who in turn whispered back. Agilaz frowned. What in Hel's domain were these people about? The guards parted then, and the apparent leader waved him forward.

Agilaz glared at the man who had kept them waiting in the cold before accepting his invitation. They escorted him through the great doors into a long hall. Footfalls echoed behind him. He stilled the urge to glance over his shoulder. Armed men were following, at least five of them.

Hermod looked back, tried to speak, but Agilaz silenced him a heavy grip on his shoulder. There was a time to acknowledge bad manners. All things had their proper time, and patience was oft the difference between wisdom and foolhardiness. The boy would learn it.

The king and his queen were both too aged, especially the former. To hold a throne so long meant he must be cunning, ruthless, or beloved. From what Agilaz had seen of the town, he doubted Nidud fell into the last category.

"Agilaz Wadeson," Nidud said. "Thegn to Jarl Hadding of the Hasdingi. Your exploits are fast becoming a legend, even here in Njarar."

Agilaz inclined his head. "King Nidud. I'm honored you've heard of me."

"Indeed. If one believes the skalds, your archery skills would make you a match for Ullr himself."

"I would never deign to compare myself to any of the Vanir."

Nidud chuckled. "How modest, archer. What do you wish here?"

To the point then. No invitation of hospitality as custom dictated—only the barest pretense of civility to one who ought to be his ally. Did the king know who he was? He knew of Agilaz's father, after all. It stood to reason he might understand the connection between Agilaz and Volund. It had been a mistake to reveal his parentage to the Aesir. If Nidud had heard his name, perhaps the dvergar might one day as well. Volund, though, he would have been wise enough not to reveal his heritage. His little brother was cunning and always wary.

Agilaz frowned and gazed about the hall. A lot of men, well-armed, and many wearing chain almost as fine as Otwin had. "Word reaches us you employ the finest craftsman in the world of Men. I would see this smith for myself and ... with your permission ... I would have him craft something for me as well."

Nidud shifted on his throne and drummed his fingers. "With my boys away at war, this place has grown too quiet. Dull. I would have some entertainment. A demonstration of your legendary skill seems in order."

"If it would please my king."

"Oh, it would." Nidud motioned, and guards encroached around Agilaz and Hermod. A pair of them grabbed his son.

Agilaz reached for his knife, but a man punched him in the gut. Gasping, he fell to his knees as they dragged Hermod away. His boy was kicking, shouting for him.

"What treachery is this?" Agilaz could barely catch his breath, and still he stumbled to his feet.

"You know the custom, I'm sure. What better way to test a man's aim than with a living target?"

The king's men marched Hermod back toward the main entrance, in the middle of the hall. One placed an apple on the boy's head. Then they backed away. Hermod stood there, jaw clenched and only the slightest tremble in his legs.

"This *game* is not played with children, but with grown warriors." And it was barbaric, often resulting in men being maimed, killed. Drunken fools and old men tired of life played it, and even then, not so far a shot.

Nidud shrugged. "It is played between those who care about the outcome. Since there is no one else here you could be expected to care for, show us your skill. You can do it, can you not? Show me you are worthy of the workings of my smith."

Agilaz glanced back and forth between his son and this vile king. What cruelty prompted such an act? Hadding was a fool to throw in with this man, no matter what he offered. And Volund ... he was here at this man's mercy. But Volund was a man grown, and Hermod was Agilaz's own son. His brother would not ask this of him under any circumstances.

"No craft is worth risking the life of my son," he said. Damn Nidud, but he could not save his brother. Not at such a cost. He'd feared to leave Hermod alone in Aujum, alone to be used or harmed by enemies Agilaz knew remained behind him. He had not considered Nidud would imagine such a mockery of hospitality. "I withdraw my request. I shall take my son and leave."

Some of the men surrounding him grumbled in disappointment. What would Hadding do on learning of Nidud's behavior? Would he consent to march against the Sviarland king? Even if he would, they could not seize this place. Such a war would be hopeless.

"It seems your prowess with a bow is exaggerated. How disappointing. Or perhaps you need more motivation?" The king rose and advanced, one shambling step at a time. "How about this then? Shoot the apple, or you both hang from the platform for, say, an hour? Does that entice you to a demonstration?"

Frey's flaming sword. The king had gone Mist-mad. Agilaz knew his mouth hung open, but he could find no words, even in his own mind. He felt empty. Blank. That, of course, was the best way to shoot.

With a long, low breath, he let his quiver slip to the floor. Then he pulled two arrows from it, one in hand, one wedged into the cracks between floor stones. He looked to Hermod.

"You can do it, Papa." The boy was not shaking any more. He had gone absolutely still.

All else fell away. The hall, the guards, the evil king. They vanished into his periphery as he nocked an arrow and drew it to his cheek. Even Hermod was gone. All that remained in the World was the apple and the arrow and his own slow, steady breath. There was naught else.

Naught else at all.

He loosed. The arrow flew straight and split the apple down the middle.

Some of the gathered men cheered, other shouted in disbelief. Dimly, he saw a few exchanging coins. They had bet on whether his son would live or not.

Nidud sank back onto his throne and clapped his hands. "Well done. Well done indeed." He shifted around as if having trouble finding comfort in his chair. "Tell me, if you could make such a shot, what was the second arrow even for?"

"For you, should any harm have come to my son." The words left his mouth before he could think better of them. So much for patience. His hands shook with cold rage.

Many of the warriors brandished spears at his words, and a collective gasp had silenced the hall.

Nidud however, snorted. "Well said. I commend your honesty. And your courage. You may see the smith—tell him to craft whatever it is you wish, archer."

Agilaz nodded, not trusting himself to speak.

HE DARED NOT LEAVE Hermod alone with the king and his men, so the boy had accompanied him into the darkness of the deep forge. Such a place seemed to belong to some Otherworld, one not meant for men to walk. Hard to even fathom his brother had ever lived and worked in dark halls like this one. Indeed, Agilaz had never understood what kind of strange life Volund must have had there. He spoke of it little.

Maybe he'd known no one could understand.

"Uncle Volund is here?" Hermod whispered.

Agilaz stiffened. Neither of his guards had reacted to the boy's words, so he had to hope they had missed them. It would not do for Nidud to learn of his relation to Volund, not now.

The guards led him to a bridge crossing an underground lake. Hermod knelt as though intent to touch the water. Agilaz snatched him up. The guards were watching them now, with wry smiles. The lake must contain some hidden danger—he'd swear to it.

At the guard house, his escort left him, pointing to the rocky island beyond the end of the bridge. They walked alone to the gap at the end. It was small enough even Hermod could make the leap. What was the point in such a gap? How could a short jump keep Volund confined here?

After patting Hermod on the shoulder, Agilaz leapt over the gap, then turned to his son. "Come. I will catch you."

The boy stepped back, then ran and jumped. Agilaz swept him into his arms, then set him down on the rocks.

"I want you to remain outside the forge. Do not go nigh

to the lake. Stay right there." He pointed to a rock pile nearby.

After glancing back and forth between the water and the forge, the boy scrambled up onto the rocks and sat there. Maybe Agilaz should have let him follow inside, but this place seemed fraught with danger, and it all left a hollow feeling in his gut. They should all of them be away from Njarar as swiftly as they could. As soon as he found Volund, he'd need to think of a way to help his brother escape.

The forge itself was dimly lit, the dancing fires seeming to magnify the shadows instead of push them aside. The place stank with sweat and coal smoke and something acidic he couldn't identify.

"Volund?"

"Brother." The voice kept to a dark corner. It sounded like him, but off. Raspier, like he had taken ill. "You ought not to have come here."

"I've come to free you."

"You cannot. Not alone."

Maybe not. Maybe he could convince Hadding to return with an army. If only he could see some way to attack the fortress other than that suicidal path to the main gate. "Surely I can do something to aid your situation."

"Perhaps." Volund stumbled into the torchlight, dragging an obviously lame leg behind him. His long hair, once bound at the nape of his neck, now hung in disheveled strands. Black strands. Even more striking, his skin had turned a sickly gray.

"B-brother? What in Hel's underworld have they done to you?"

"Not *her* underworld, I think. They woke something, something the dvergar perhaps planted in me."

Agilaz's legs threatened to give out from beneath him.

He stumbled backward until he collided with a workbench, then leaned against it to steady himself.

"What is it, brother?" Volund asked. "Do you not like the monster that stands before you? Does my likeness frighten you?" His brother chuckled then, as though let in on some jest Agilaz could not begin to fathom.

"Are you ..." Agilaz swallowed. There was a tale, a vicious rumor he and Slagfid had promised never to speak of again. Knowledge was precious, but on rare occasions a man was better off not knowing things. Or so Slagfid had thought, and he was the eldest brother. But then, perhaps stumbling in ignorance might prove worse. "Are you certain the dvergar put it in you?"

Volund shrugged, an elaborate motion that swayed not only his hair, but the very shadows around it. A trick of the firelight, was all. Aught more was impossible. Was madness.

"Father never brought your mother to court," Agilaz said. "There were stories ... he had met some woman in the woods and lain with her. That in the middle of one night, in the dead of winter, she had come back. Left you on his doorstep. A skald once claimed a slave had seen the woman and she seemed inhuman, like some vaettr. But if this slave existed, no one found her. And father did not speak of such things."

A thoughtful look fell over Volund's face, and then he melted back into shadows so thick Agilaz could not make out his form. This was a place of nightmares. Maybe Volund was right; maybe he should have never come here. But he had done so. And this king had *lamed* his brother.

"Tell me what I can do to help you."

"They took my ring, brother. Altvir's ring. I would have it back." The disembodied voice sent the hairs on the back of his neck standing on it. Praise be to Frey he had not brought

Hermod in here. The boy would have had nightmares for a moon or more. As, Agilaz suspected, would Hermod's father.

"Who has it?"

"The princess, Bodvild. Ask her to meet me in secret. She will have seen the jewelry I've crafted. Tell her I would make something for her. Tell her whatever will get her here —but I must see her, brother."

Agilaz shuddered. "I will tell her."

Maybe Altvir's ring would help Volund escape this place. Agilaz hoped so. Because he wanted to be gone, as well. Far away.

21

DAYS GONE

Two Years Ago

*T*he winter would break soon. A moon, perhaps, and the ice on the lake would begin to melt. They all wanted to take advantage before that. The three valkyries skated about the lake, laughing, shaping complex patterns with one another as though weaving a tapestry.

Agilaz's young son, Hermod, clapped his hands, vainly chasing after his mother, one way and the next. In their graceful dance, the valkyries managed to somehow avoid colliding even with the ungainly child. This was his third winter, and he could barely keep his feet on the skates. Agilaz shouted advice at his son, still not quite able to appreciate the moment.

Or maybe he did in his own way, Volund supposed. Certainly he wanted what was best for his son. From the time he was born, and every few moons thereafter, Agilaz had crafted a new fur jerkin for Hermod. Volund's brother hunted down wolves, deer, even a cave hyena once. That pack had wandered into the valley and sparked a pitched struggle for territory with the dire wolves. The wolves were better than hyenas, so Agilaz had hunted more than a few of the nasty animals to give the wolves an edge. Since then, the wolves seemed to have settled into an uneasy truce with the brothers.

Altvir leapt into the air, using a beat of wings that vanished an instant later to carry her halfway across the lake. Volund skated in that direction, shaking his head. She was showing off, which was something he expected more from Svanhit than his own wife. Still, Altvir was a strange one, never quite predictable. She had convinced her sister valkyries to marry the brothers, and to this day, seven winters later, he could not quite say why. He could say only that he loved her. And that these years were the first in his life he'd known true peace.

Olrun caught her son in her arms and spun around, sending a sheen of frost spraying from her skates. The boy laughed.

"Papa! Papa!"

And Agilaz was smiling. Just a little.

That seemed a miracle, after all.

MIDNIGHT HAD PASSED, and still Altvir and he sat upon the frozen lakeshore, a torch stuck in the ground nearby. His arse was cold, but he hadn't found himself wanting to rise. Or not wholly. Yes, the house promised warmth and the peaceful escape of dreams. He liked to dream these days. In dreams, sometimes he walked with a child's hand in his own. Except on waking, he would realize the child did not exist. Maybe never would.

Altvir had not pushed him to go in, had not even asked.

She could sense his moods, sure enough. Perhaps she even knew what he dwelt on, though she had not spoken of it. Indeed, she seemed far away, her attention ever drawn to the north.

Finally Volund sighed. "What has happened?"

Altvir shook her head.

"Tell me."

She rose then, and folded her arms across her chest. "I'm trying to protect you."

"You cannot protect me from the truth, especially if it weighs on you."

"I can *try*."

Volund frowned. She must have sensed wars. Men dying in battle, some meeting heroic ends. Their urd. And those who ought to have valkyries claiming their souls, taking them to Valhalla. Did some of them linger, trapped as shades or drawn down toward Hel because the brothers had taken valkyries from their duties? From the oaths they had made to whatever eldritch power they served? They did not speak of their mistress, save once an intimation that even *she* served yet another—the true force that held them bound. Those rings had been gifts from the Otherworlds, as were the wings. The valkyries' oaths held them somewhere between life and death, somewhere between Man and vaettr. That much he had garnered.

Other troubles, concerns, had come to bother him much more than those secrets. He did not blame Altvir for holding some truths deep inside. He did the same, rarely choosing to speak of his time in Nidavellir. He had told her once he feared they had done something to him. The look of sadness in her eyes had kept from saying more.

"Another battle?"

"There's always another."

War was a constant. Such was the way of the World. Volund just grunted. "Hermod liked skating."

"Certainly so." She smiled, still seeming far away.

"It makes me wonder ..."

"Volund ..."

"How, after seven years of marriage, does only one couple have a child?"

Altvir sighed and turned away, again staring off to the north. No doubt one petty king preyed upon the land of another. The dvergar claimed Mankind was slowly dying out, an eventuality they wished to prevent. Without Mankind, they had no hosts in this Realm. Sometimes they spoke of waging wars of conquest merely to put a stop to Men from killing themselves. If all Mankind were enslaved, the race might stand to live out the next few centuries, or so Durin and others had argued. But the dvergar never seemed to convince their king to act. They did naught quickly, for they had long memories of their battles with the Vanir and the Old Kingdoms like the Niflungar and the Lofdar. Some of their foes were steeped enough in sorcery to pose a threat to dvergar, to cast them out of this Realm entirely. They were not keen to risk what they had without due consideration.

And so instead they dwelt in their debauchery and isolation, passing the ages by as the World faded around them.

"You've grown morose." She was looking back at him now.

"I would have sons." Olrun's pregnancy had run long, but perhaps that was because she was a valkyrie.

"Only sons?"

"Or daughters, too." He strode out to her on the ice and wrapped his arm around her shoulders. "Children of my own to raise and carry on my legacy."

"Meaning?"

Meaning he would teach them his craft, of course. Or did she imply that to learn his arts would require them endure what he had? If the dvergar were right, if a crafter must himself or herself be tempered first ... No. No, if that be the case, the knowledge would die with him. Mortal arts were enough, and he could teach those as well. He would visit no suffering upon his children. Never.

"Perhaps I am barren," she said before he had formed an answer.

He turned her about to look in her eyes. Still luminous green, and glistening with the hint of unshed tears. She never shed tears, but then, he could not remember seeing her like this. "Is that the truth? Could you not conceive were you so inclined? You and Svanhit both?"

"Svanhit perhaps fears Slagfid's heart is less true than it might be."

Volund felt like he'd been slapped. He released Altvir and stepped backward. His brother might be flighty, but he had never been unfaithful. Not as far as Volund knew. For that matter, Svanhit was herself mercurial. "Do you think that of me, that my love for you is tainted?"

"N-no. I didn't mean that." Altvir rubbed her forehead as if in pain. "Volund, I—"

"Well, what did you mean, wife? Have you some doubt about me? Am I not worthy to sire your children?"

"Suppose your unspoken fears hold merit." The tears in her eyes had gone, replaced with a hollow light barely escaping through her narrowed lids. "What if a seed of darkness were planted in you in the deep kingdom? Could not that seed be carried in *your* seed?"

Volund shook his head. No. Impossible. She had burned the darkness out of him. He was safe, he was pure. And she was saying she had not borne him a child for fear of his own nature. "You trust me so little."

"I have trusted you so *very* much, Volund. More than you can know."

"And yet you wound me!" He took another step away. Not quite able to look at her. How could he do so, knowing she believed such vileness ran through his veins? And could she be right? Could there still linger within him such a horror?

Now she looked down, shaking her head, refusing to meet his gaze. "It was not my intention."

And now he had somehow become the villain here, hurt *her*. Hel take him for it. Hesitantly, he returned to her side and knelt before her. Took her hand in his own. "I pledged myself to you. If you ever deign to give me a child, I shall rejoice. But either way, I love you, strange creature though you are. In spite of it, because of it, I cannot see myself without your light."

"Oh," Altvir pulled him to his feet and into an embrace so tight it hurt, "I wish I could tell you the weight of my oath."

"Then *do* tell me." He whispered in her ear, patting her hair.

"Come. Let's go to bed."

22

VOLUND

*S*omeone has come.

Oh, yes. They had been pleased with the gifts. In fact, the queen had so loved the brooches, she had ordered fresh venison and ale delivered to him in reward. Now they would ask him to craft more finery for them. Perhaps this time he would make boots out of Thakkrad's skin.

Kill them all.

Oh, vengeance demanded more than death. To kill the king and queen would be quick, relatively painless for them. No, for their crimes they needed to suffer the rest of their days. One day, one day very soon, they would need to learn what he had done to their sons. By now, they probably had begun to wonder where the boys had gotten off to. Perhaps they thought them gone off to the wars, seeking glory. Certainly that had been Ulf's intent.

"Hello?" The feminine voice was young, timid.

Oh. Agilaz had done his work, then. It was too perfect. Finally, at long last, all the pieces had begun to fall together.

The fire was hot enough now, the forge stoked. The last step in his revenge walked in, freely, on her own two legs.

Sadly, off in the wars, Nidud's eldest son was beyond Volund's reach, but his daughter, the queen's precious favorite—she would do.

Cane in hand, Volund hobbled to stand nigh to the forge entrance. The girl strolled in, looking all about as though the deep forge were some tapestry to be inspected for conversation over the night meal. She had blonde hair, like her brothers, but longer, hanging freely about her neck in the fashion of maids and unmarried girls. Tall for a girl, too, tall as he was.

"Hello?" She started as he stepped closer. "You're the smith, Volund?"

Volund nodded, but kept to the shadows beyond the firelight. His appearance had disturbed the boys, and he could not afford to spook this girl. "Forgive me for not coming out to meet you. I do not walk so well these days, you see."

"Oh! What happened?"

At that he flinched. By the fathomless darkness of Svartalfheim! She was serious. She had lived in this castle and somehow not heard her father had publicly maimed him. What did that mean? The obvious answer would be one— or both—of her parents had gone to some lengths to keep her in the dark. To let her think them innocent, hide their heinous crimes. That made using her less tasteful. Still, if the king and queen had taken such effort to keep their daughter innocent, they must favor her greatly. And in the end, what hurt most was losing that which you held most precious.

Take it. Take it all from them. Let them see how it feels to be bereft of hope and cast into the infinite night of despair.

Volund grimaced. What must be, would be.

"Why are you here, girl?"

"Bodvild. I'm Princess Bodvild."

"Yes, you are."

She strolled about the forge now, peering at the tools. She paused by a table and picked up an ivory-handled dagger. The hilt was carved from her little brother's thighbone. She did not seem to notice. "I heard you made those beautiful brooches for my mother."

Volund smiled. "Oh yes. I enjoyed crafting those immensely."

He too began to move, hobbling a step closer to the firelight, making certain to keep himself between her and the exit. One hand on the cane, another brushing over the hilt of a knife at his belt.

"I knew it! When you look at that kind of detail you can just see the love that went into them. I always thought that, after all. That the finest works could only be made by someone who loves his craft."

"Hmmm. I could not agree more, princess." He continued forward, but she had her back to him, didn't see.

"They always refused to let me come down here before. I don't know why. This time though, I couldn't resist. I had to sneak down on my own."

"And you want me to make something for you." Or from you.

She turned, smiling, a smile that faltered when she saw his ashen skin and onyx hair. "What happened to you?"

Volund chuckled and leaned on his cane. Hel, if she only knew the answer to that. He'd been traded to dvergar by his father in an ill-conceived ploy that cost him everything. Traded, tortured. Tempered. That was the word. A process that had continued. Bodvild's father had accomplished what even the legendary Dvalin had not. He had brought out the darkness in Volund's veins, lifted it to the surface such that it was laid plain. And still, they did not know what they saw. Perhaps they convinced themselves he had always been dark, swarthy, unlike them. Perhaps allowed themselves to believe the forge alone had changed their prisoner.

They were fools. If Volund had any doubt left as to the truth, Agilaz's tale of his birth had shattered that doubt.

And now, it took the innocence of this girl to ask the question grown men and warriors dared not, fearing the answer.

You stand upon the threshold now.

He clucked his tongue. What had happened to him indeed? "You know ... I think my mother may have been a foreigner."

"You mean from Serkland, or ... or somewhere beyond the Midgard Wall?"

Volund nodded and continued closer, until he could almost feel the warmth of her skin. "Beyond it, yes, I think so. Farther than Serkland, I'd wager."

"By Freyja. She must have quite the stories to tell. No one lets me travel anywhere. I saw the town once, it was amazing. All those people each with their own lives, trades. That must be so interesting, to have a trade."

"Hmmm." His mother would have had stories to tell, had he ever met her.

Finish it.

Perhaps one day he still might meet the woman. Was it lust that had driven her to take up with Wade? Or had she had some deliberate plot, a ploy to saddle Kvenland with a bastard son who was not quite whole? If dvergar could make moves planned out centuries ahead, could not all vaettir take such actions? If he was a piece on a tafl board, was he then a pawn? Or as a prince, was he a more valuable piece? He tended to think the latter.

"So, you make jewelry?"

"I can make most aught you might wish."

Bodvild held out her hand, displaying a tarnished ring. It had grown so plain, he had almost not even recognized Altvir's band. Only the slightest hint of its luster still shone where once it had glittered in the light. "You made this one, right? But it's losing its quality, and I can't see why. I tried having it polished, but it can't be fixed."

Volund's hand trembled as he reached for the ring. "I did not make that one." His voice sounded so hollow, weak in his own ears. Empty, like the ring without its sheen.

Bodvild pulled her hand back as if suddenly wary. Far too late for it, of course.

Step over the threshold.

The threshold? Oh, but he knew what they would have him do. This girl was but a means to that end. And still, it tasted foul in his mouth. She was not her mother.

Step over the threshold and be free. Or linger forever in twilight.

Was that his urd? To not quite embrace the darkness and still be shunned and blinded by the light? No. He was meant for a grander urd than that. And if the only way forward was through darkness, then it was darkness he must become.

Volund motioned to a stein of ale that sat on a table. "Join me in a drink?"

"Oh, I don't know … I just wanted to get my ring fixed."

Volund poured some ale into a goblet and offered it to her. "I thought you wished to hear of the lives of others. I can tell you quite a tale, you know. Stories you would not believe. You know, I have visited the deep kingdom."

"Nidavellir?" Bodvild took the goblet without taking her

eyes off his face. She settled in a chair and sipped, her attention so rapt he could almost feel it on her skin.

Do not turn away.

Volund sunk down into another chair with a groan.
"Nidavellir, yes. The Otherworld of the dvergar."

"Dwarves?" She giggled.

"Mmmm. The dvergar are experts on suffering, you
know. Their very existence is predicated upon it. They can
neither walk nor sit without pain. After long enough like
that, it sometimes seems the only respite from their pain
comes from inflicting it on others."

"Oh!" She hiccuped and swayed in her chair. "Well, that
sounds awful. I shouldn't like to meet them."

"No. I suppose you wouldn't." Volund swallowed and let
his forehead slump into his palm. Finally, he looked up at
her through his now-black hair. She was sipping more. "To
deal with their pain, they cultivate mushrooms that have a
mind-altering effect on their mortal hosts. Sapphire
shrooms, they call them."

"Uh. I feel funny."

"The dvergar built this place, too. These mushrooms
grow down here, in the dank gloom where so few things can
thrive. And if you're not used to them, I fear they can prove
quite powerful."

Bodvild tried to stand and instead toppled over backward. She lay on the stone floor, staring at the forge roof.
What did she see? The play of shadows? Or perhaps brilliant colors born of her own imagination. A rainbow of
sensation.

Standing was hard, of course. His leg protested, but less
than he expected, as if her suffering had somehow fed him.
In such a case, it became harder than ever to deny his

course. He shuffled over and knelt above her, knife in hand. There it was, on her finger.

A ring that bound him to Altvir. And in giving it to another, the foul queen had robbed that ring of its glory. The last of its luster had winked out, yet he had to believe it still held power. Maybe enough power for him to free himself from this place.

The freedom is in vengeance. Become who you are.

Volund sighed. "Your father had me abducted. He stole that which I valued most. Tortured me. Maimed me. And so I cut down your brothers. In doing so I regained some small measure of my strength, my vitality. Or perhaps I unlocked what had lain dormant there all along. It is in me, girl. And your life might complete my vengeance, and evoke the depths of that power, and with it, my freedom."

There are worse things than murder. Do not turn away. Walk into darkness, or dwindle to naught in half-light.

Volund's hands shook. He looked at the ring, faded and hopeless as himself. Only complete vengeance would balance the scales and finally waken the seed within him.

And but one path remained to him.

With the knife, he cut away the girl's dress.

23

AGILAZ

*K*ing Nidud of Njarar had at last deigned to feed Agilaz and Hermod. Their feast hall lay across from his throne room. A dozen braziers and a great hearth lit the room and provided warmth. Even the distance from the main hall did not quite abolish the howl of the wind outside. Summer was well under way, true, but a chill rain had risen.

In all honesty, Agilaz would have preferred to leave and seek shelter in the town below the mountain. With the rainstorm, though, it was too late for that. And if Nidud had not offered him hospitality he didn't know what he'd have done for Hermod. The boy ate ravenously. Agilaz found it a bit hard to stomach food from the table of a man who had hamstrung his brother and, worse, threatened his son.

By now, most like, the princess had paid a visit to Volund. And if he had stolen back the ring, perhaps he had escaped. If so, Agilaz too needed to be away from here. Despite the risk, he might have to try to take Hermod and sneak out in the night. If they could make it off the mountain, he could lose the Njararans. The storm would even work in his favor, though it would prove hard on poor Hermod. The boy was strong, though—he had more than proved that.

"So tell me, archer," Nidud said. "What did you request of my smith?"

Agilaz took a long swallow of ale. He should have prepared an answer for such a question already, but the shock of seeing Volund like that ... "Well, my king." Agilaz took another sip. Only one answer came to mind. "An archer is naught without well-wrought arrows."

"Oh, indeed. And is he making arrows for you now?"

Agilaz opened his mouth. The loud caw of a raven rang through the feast hall, interrupting him.

The bird had perched above the hearth, though Agilaz had not noticed it fly in.

The queen put a hand to her chest and shook her head, as though the shock had almost been too much for her.

Several of the thegns at the table murmured, and a slave rushed over to wave the bird away.

"I think—" Agilaz began.

The raven cawed again. As the slave drew nigh, the raven swooped at the man. A swift peck of its beak tore out one of the slave's eyes. The man fell screaming, clutching his face.

Agilaz launched himself to his feet, fumbling to get his bow off his back.

The raven spat out the eye and laughed. Not the laugh of a bird, but of a man. Its dark chuckle rang through the hall and sent shivers through Agilaz.

"What sorcery?" Nidud demanded.

"Do you sleep well, lord of the Njarar?" the raven asked ... in Volund's raspy voice.

A terrible cold settled over Agilaz.

The king rose slowly, steadying himself on the table. "I-I do not."

"Nor ought you, son of Man, he who thought to imprison a prince of the alfar. Do your sons fare well now? Was it wise to send them to fight your battles?"

"What are you?"

It was a nightmare. He had but to wake from it.

The raven cackled. "You ought to have asked that before cutting my leg, oh mighty king."

"Volund? How is this ..." The king held up his hands as if to ward off evil.

Agilaz was half inclined to do the same. Volund had taken the ring, he must have. And somehow it had let him change his form, as their wives did. With a hand beneath the table, Agilaz began to draw Hermod away. They needed to be free from here, and quickly. Whatever Volund intended, it did not seem to bode well for them. Not for anyone.

"Why do you speak of my boys, Volund?" the king demanded. "What has become of my sons?"

Volund cackled again. "A great many things have become of them, king. Go to the deep forge and see for yourself. See the bellows spattered in blood where I hacked their heads from their shoulders. Dredge the lake and find their limbs. Even now, you drink from a goblet carved from one's skull, inlaid with silver."

Nidud paled, his eyes dropping the ivory cup on the table. The queen looked down at a similar goblet before her and screamed.

"Oh, cunning wife of Nidud," Volund said when she quieted. "Do you not like the goblet? And yet you wear their teeth upon your breast."

Oh, Hel. The brooch? What had Volund done?

Volund snickered again, the sound deafening in the now silent hall. Agilaz tried to pull Hermod away, but the boy was shaking. Damn Volund for letting his son see such horror.

"And dear Bodvild, your precious daughter. Already my seed has taken root in her womb. I think mine like to be the only child she ever bears."

The queen collapsed to the floor, babbling and pointing at the raven that now flew about the chamber.

"Live in despair, king," Volund said. "And know that when death closes in around you, I shall wait on the other side to drag your soul to the gates of Hel. Or somewhere *darker*."

Nidud swallowed hard, turning empty eyes on Agilaz. "Shoot it. Shoot the monster!"

He couldn't move at all. He couldn't think, couldn't act.

This was impossible.

"Kill him or your lives are forfeit, archer!"

Nidud was right. The king was a monster—but so was Volund. He had murdered two princes and raped the princess, all so he could release that monster from deep inside himself. All so he could become this accursed thing. And still he was his brother.

Agilaz nocked an arrow. The raven swooped past him, out into the main hall.

"Papa!" Hermod shrieked.

Men were advancing on him, swords and spears readied. The nearest, Nidud's thegn Thakkrad, had snatched Hermod by the arm. Agilaz swerved and loosed his arrow. It punched through Thakkrad's eye and sent him crashing into the table, overturning all the dishes.

"Run, son!" he shouted.

Hermod did so, dashing for the main hall. Agilaz ran

several steps after him, then turned to face the charging troops. He launched an arrow into the throat of the nearest one, then raced out again in the chaos.

A guard lay on the floor, clutching his face. The raven had torn out another eye. Hermod raced out of the hall, ducking under a guard's arms and sliding outside. There was no way Agilaz had time to get any more shots off now. His foes were too close. He tossed the bow aside and pulled a knife from his belt, then slammed bodily into the guard who'd tried to grab his son.

The man toppled to the ground, and Agilaz leapt over him. Shouts echoed through the hall. A spearman blocking the exit thrust at him. The man was shocked by the scene, must have been—his attack was clumsy. Agilaz stepped around it and caught the spear in one hand. He flung himself forward and buried the knife in his attacker's armpit.

As the spearman fell, Agilaz wrested the weapon from him. He spun on the others. They advanced in a rough unit now, several with shields up. Agilaz backed outside, into the pouring rain.

A glance over his shoulder, all he could spare. Hermod was backing away, toward the edge of the platform. Lightning crashed above, silhouetting the boy.

Agilaz's ring had grown warm. Yes, he would see his love very soon. If this did not qualify as a valorous death, he knew not what would. A dozen men advanced, forcing him to fall back. Others already blocked the path, denying him even the barest hope of escape.

"Stay behind me!" Agilaz shouted. "And whatever happens, do not cower. Meet the end on your feet and you may see Valhalla!"

Men surged forward. Agilaz flung the knife in one's face.

He saw it coming too late, didn't start to raise his shield in time. The blade hit between his eyes and one of his companions tripped over his falling body. Agilaz ducked to the side and slammed his shoulder into the shield of another. The man lost his footing and fell backward over the platform, screaming.

A blade bit into Agilaz's ribs and something hard slammed into his face. The impact bowled him over and sent him sliding along the rain-slicked platform until his head dangled over open space.

"Papa!"

More thunder. Crashing. Demanding more from him before the end.

His ring had become a molten flame on his hand. He would die on his feet, and she would come for him. If he had but one last wish, it would to be look into those pale blue eyes of hers one more time. Agilaz roared as he rolled to his feet. Unarmed, he did the only thing he could and flung his own body into the nearest man.

Something sharp gouged his shoulder. It did not matter. Lightning flashed. He grabbed the man and hurled him out behind himself, into the open air. Thunder covered his screams.

Men before him faltered. They knew they would buy his death dearly. Skalds would speak of this day.

Lightning nigh blinded him even as a heavy impact crashed onto the platform, flinging standing water up in a wave that washed out in all directions. Every man there froze, blinking away the afterimages of the lightning.

A silver-winged woman rose from a crouch, sword in hand. With terrifying swiftness she surged at a pair of men. Her sword lopped off one's head while she caught the other by the throat. With one hand she flung him out, off the platform and into the night. Those screams rang for a long time.

The woman, the valkyrie, looked to him ... with those beautiful, pale blue eyes.

Was he dead? Had that last blow felled him? He looked down, but blood still seeped from his wounds.

"Mama!"

Hermod's voice tore him from the dream, and Agilaz caught the boy in his arms, shielding him with his own body.

Olrun folded her arms over her chest and swept her wings together. Their beat hurled her off the platform and created a wave of air that flung Nidud's men backward, into the great hall. A moment later, strong arms caught Agilaz around the waist, and he and Hermod were swept up.

Air scoured his face as they plummeted downward faster than a man could fall. Each beat of Olrun's silver wings carried them uncounted fathoms away from the castle and out into the night. Her chest heaved with the effort of carrying them. On she pushed, farther.

He called to her, but the wind swallowed his words.

Until the ground began surging toward them.

"Olrun!" he shouted.

Trees drew nigh. All he could do was tighten his grip on Hermod. They brushed over the treetops and out into a clearing.

Not a clearing, he saw below them. A lake.

He had time for no other thought before they plunged into the chilling waters.

THE SMALL FIRE might attract attention. Agilaz could see no way around that risk. Hermod was shivering and had to get dry. And Olrun would no doubt survive, but she had lost consciousness when they hit the water. Her wings had vanished then, making it much easier to pull her from the lake.

For a long time he sat there, hand on her shoulder. His other arm was wrapped around Hermod, who had fallen asleep against him, the boy's fingers interwoven with those of his mother.

Agilaz sighed, finally able to breathe. Olrun's hair hung in a heavy braid over her shoulder, but strands had come loose, either in their flight, or underwater. Agilaz ran a hand over her cheek as she stirred, blinking. Those beautiful eyes.

"You came back for us."

Olrun pushed herself up. "Well, I ..."

"I thought you would come for my soul."

She glanced around until she spied her sword where he had stuck it in the mud. "That was the plan. That was what I was supposed to do."

"You could not watch us die."

Olrun swallowed and looked up at the sky. "They do not like us to bear children."

He could see why not. He had never known a mother to turn her back on her children. Not for any rule, not for any law.

After laying Hermod on the ground, he rose to his feet, then helped her stand as well. "I will not let you go again, wife."

"I gave you all the years I could. The oath always draws me away."

No. He shook his head. He would not accept that. "I will chase you down, again and again, mother of my son. Love of my life. I will track you across Midgard and ... if you so force me, beyond. Through all the wilds of Utgard if need be." He held up his hand, displaying her ring. "I will never give up on you."

Olrun pressed her palms to her temples. "Oh, Agilaz. What you want is not how it works."

He pointed at Hermod. "Tell that to our son."

"He would be our *only* child."

"Why? You spoke once of wanting a daughter."

She bit her lip, then shook her head. "My mistress punished me for giving you the first child. I will never be able to bear another." She put a hand on his shoulder and squeezed. "You are a prince. Go! Find some princess to love and let her give you a dozen children. Live your life."

Now he shook his head. "Not without you. You are the only princess I care for."

Her expression warred between joy and grief, until finally, she looked up at the sky once again. "Is this truly what you want?"

"You know it is. You've always known. No oath you ever made or could make counts for more than the one between husband and wife."

Olrun shivered such that he could barely stop himself from throwing his arms around her. The cold was probably not the cause of her distress. "Agilaz ... you must return to me the ring of my mistress."

He hesitated. That ring was all that had let him follow her. If he handed it over and she chose to flee, he could not pursue.

"Trust me."

Trust. He asked her for a lifetime, and that meant naught without trust. His chest clenched as he slipped the band from his finger, but he did so and dropped it in her palm.

She stood there, looking at it. The moonlight reflected off the coppery band. Then she shut her eyes and set her jaw. When she opened them, she strode to her sword and took it up.

Was that it? Was she going?

She met his gaze.

And she set the ring upon a rock. "You will have to give me a new wedding band, one day soon."

"What are you—"

"Stand back." She held her sword before her face, whispering something.

A long time she stood like that, speaking some tongue he could not begin to catch, much less understand. Until the first rays of the rising sun began to reflect off her sword blade. Then she raised the blade above her head. Her silver wings shot from her back and spread into the sky. With a shriek, she thrust the sword downward. It pierced the ring and rock both, burying itself.

The ground rumbled outward from that rock. Hermod woke from it, but Agilaz wrapped his cloak around the boy, shielding him. Olrun's whole body shook. She turned to him, light pouring from her eyes and mouth and nose. The earthquake built in intensity.

The ring melted into the stone. The sword turned to glass and shattered in her hands. And then her wings exploded. It hit him in a wave of heat and light that flung him to the ground and sent him tumbling end over end. Dazed, he lay there a moment.

What the ...

Gods! Olrun!

A macabre spray of blood and swan feathers covered the

lakeside and floated upon the water. Olrun lay face down in the mud, clad in naught but her undershirt, now soaked through with crimson. The armor had vanished, trails of gold melted into the ground. No obvious wound marred her, but her back was drenched in blood.

"Olrun!"

"Mama!"

He and Hermod raced to her side, rolled her over.

Her chest rose and fell lightly. She lived.

Agilaz kissed her face, her forehead, her lips. Hermod wept over his mother.

24

SLAGFID

They had taken respite in the völva's dome, spent the night there. The Niflung assassin had not come for them. That provided very little comfort, for the völva claimed he had passed the night in sorcery, had summoned aid to himself.

Slagfid had been too afraid to ask what kind of aid a sorcerer assassin might call on. Naught good, naught meant to walk on Midgard.

At first light they had pressed on, down the mountain and into the woods. They would not make the town. Not unless Guthorm paused to examine the tomb. Kelda had begged the völva to come with them. The witch had refused, said she would rather meet her end on a Niflung blade than succumb to her age climbing a mountain. Slagfid did not blame her. It was the most honorable death he could offer her, though he doubted any valkyrie would come for the old völva. What urd did that leave her? To descend to reach the gates of Hel, or else to remain, trapped in torment as a shade haunting this place. He did not blame her, but nor did he envy her.

Panting, Kelda paused, leaning against a tree. None of the others looked much better. No sleep for two days, and now they'd all but run down a mountain. Terror of the impending sunset kept them standing, but not much more.

"We do not have much time, princess." Slagfid looked at the sky. No sign of the sun, hard to judge the proper time. "They will be upon us soon."

"And we cannot outrun them. Let us at least choose the terms we will fight on."

By the ghosts of his ancestors, he admired her grit. Maybe valkyries would not come for the völva, but they'd come for Kelda and her people. It was a shallow comfort. They had believed in him. He'd killed a Niflung and somehow, they had trusted when he promised to kill eight more. Instead, these people were all like to die to a single one of the sorcerers. Slagfid might have overcome another sorcerer by himself, but the völva said the bastard had aid now.

They could leave the path, try to hide in the woods. It was a chance, if a poor one. He could see only one alternative left. No one had questioned when he had taken Hrunting and slung it over his shoulder. Several moons training together had left no doubt he was the finest swordsman among them. They thought he could use it to save them. He supposed he would, in a way.

He unslung the sword and offered it to Kelda. "It is the legacy of your people, princess. Moreover, if the Niflungar take a runeblade, they grow that much closer to rebuilding their kingdom. You cannot let it fall into their hands. My brother told me of these swords, of the power and terrible urds they bestow on their wielders. I wanted to spare you the latter because I ..." Care for her? What did it matter now? "But no man can change his urd. And yours is to take

Hrunting and escape the Niflungar, ensure it is wielded by heroes of your people and not by some sorcerer assassin."

She took the sword and stared down at it as if a serpent writhed in her hands. "What are you saying? We will fight him together."

Slagfid sighed. That sounded wonderful. And impossible. "More than our lives are at stake here. If the sword is gone, they might not further trouble your island. Either way, you cannot let them take it. Go from this island, fast as you can, and spread the word that the Niflungar are on the move. That the old world wakens and seeks to conquer the new."

"And what will you do, prince?"

He shook his head. "I promised you eight more lives. You —and your seven men and women." It had not been what he meant. But maybe Njord would accept the offering just the same. If not, well ... fuck the damn Vanr. "Take your lives and go, push as hard as you can. Find a way off this island."

Kelda looked at her companions, must have seen how badly they wanted to flee. Oh, they would have stayed, he had no doubt. Had the princess asked them, they would have stayed, defended her. Died to the last. But they did not wish to die. Slagfid could not solve all their problems with the Niflungar. But if he had any choice in the matter, they would see at least one more dawn.

The princess slung the runeblade over her shoulder, then grabbed him and kissed him. And then she left, they all left.

Left him time to prepare. Time to pray.

⚓

ON HIS KNEES, Slagfid draw a dagger across his palm. He squeezed his fist until blood welled between his fingers, then flung it into the bonfire.

"This is the only sacrifice I have to offer. That and myself. My life, Njord, if you but protect the others. Spare them from the mist and its children."

The sun had set, and that mist grew denser. The flames kept it from engulfing him. Nearby, his sword waited for him, stuck in the ground. Kelda had once granted him that sword to fulfill his oath, to protect her people. Had he done a better job of it, he might not find himself here now. Or perhaps the gods had willed it this way. Either way, a raven watched him from the nearest tree.

That tree's branches had sprouted no leaves in the summer. It had become a husk, a hollow shell of its former self. Like the Niflungar—a people who had died out and didn't seem to know it. Much of the World had forgotten them, but now they rose once more.

Leaves crunched behind him. Slagfid rose and drew his sword in one motion. A figure stepped out of the mist. To call it a Man did it too much justice, though once it had been. Its flesh had turned sallow, its eyes glowing red beneath an iron helm. The draug clutched an axe in both hands. Perhaps the dead had no need for shields.

Another figure stepped from the mist, this one also a draug, a shieldmaiden. She bore both shield and sword. It might have been better had she worn a helm, for at least it would have partially concealed her face. A blade had severed the lower half of her jaw, exposing her rotting palate and throat.

"This is the aid you summoned, Guthorm?"

The mist congealed to his side, and he turned as a living man walked from it. He was young, or seemed it, with blond hair bound at the nape of his neck. His eyes did not glow, though a fell hunger seemed to reflect from them. "How do you know my name?"

"Not everyone has forgotten your people."

"Good." He drew a blade belted at his side. The sword glimmered in the firelight. Runes lined it, runes glowing with the barest hint of blue light. So, this assassin bore the runeblade of the Niflungar—Gramr. Guthorm followed his gaze to the runes. "Witness the final days of the age of Man."

Slagfid took one slow-paced step after another, trying to get his foes all on one side. "You believe yourself immune to Gramr's curse?"

At that the assassin prince paused, then crooked a smile. "Oh. You *know* of the runeblades? Then perhaps you even know why I am here. Hand over the blade and pledge your service, and you may yet live."

"Go back to Hel."

Guthorm shook his head. "Then you will see our lady soon enough, for there is none greater. And through her, I shall raise your corpse and bind your soul." He pointed the blade at the female draug. "You will serve me for eternity, even as your soul screams in agony and withers into oblivion."

Slagfid had no desire for more words with this sorcerer. He rushed the axe-wielding draug. The creature raised its weapon for an overhead chop. It was fast, especially for such a heavy weapon, and Slagfid barely managed to dodge to the side. He raked his sword along the draug's ribs. Though his strike bit flesh, the draug barely slowed. It twisted, making a horizontal chop that forced Slagfid to leap backward.

Already the dead shieldmaiden charged him, while Guthorm had vanished into the mists again.

"Coward!"

Slagfid rolled to the side and came up swinging at the female. She smashed his blade aside with her shield and swung overhand at him. Slagfid twisted out of the way and swept his sword low, scoring a hit on her leg. It clanked off bone and the woman stumbled. Slagfid kicked her forward, sending her toppling into the male. They knew how to use their weapons, but these were no master warriors.

The sudden whoosh from the mist was his only warning as Guthorm appeared from nowhere, swinging. Slagfid stumbled backward, parried, and tried to turn the parry into a riposte. Guthorm twisted his swing into a thrust, forcing Slagfid back again. The runeblade scraped his left shoulder. Immediately a vile chill shot through his arm. It spread with every beat of his heart, like a viper's venom, numbing him down to the hand.

He fell away, desperately parrying with his right hand. Here, he had found a master. The Niflung's relentless assault gave no room to even think of attack. Behind him, the draugar had risen and were flanking Slagfid.

Guthorm fell short then, and—before he could think better of it—Slagfid took the opening, attacking. The Niflung prince twisted out of the way and cleaved down onto Slagfid's blade. The maneuver stripped Slagfid's sword from his hand.

Slagfid leapt backward an instant before Guthorm would have opened his gut. The prince advanced on him, sword held high, aggressive. Draugar moved in on him from either side. Not much longer now.

Njord, please let Kelda have made it far from here. Let her see another dawn. Slagfid drew a knife from his belt and turned, trying to keep each opponent in view.

The male draug closed in first, with a wide horizontal

swing intended to cleave Slagfid's legs from his torso. Rather than dodge away, he dove forward, rolled under the attack, and slammed his knife into the draug's knee. The dead thing roared at him but did not fall. Fuck. Didn't feel pain, not the way a Man did.

He scrambled between the creature's legs and struggled to regain his feet, even as the creature turned about—admittedly with less grace than before. Slagfid grabbed the axe haft before the draug could strike again. Had to wrest it from the draug.

It swung the axe, flinging him to the ground on his wounded shoulder. He barely felt the impact, but he thought he heard something snap. By the ghosts of his ancestors, that fiend was strong. Even had he had two working hands, he could not have overpowered it.

"You fight well," Guthorm said, continuing his advance. He held up a hand and both draugar paused, glowing red eyes locked on Slagfid. "Well enough, but like a man who only knows how to fight the living. Years of training have honed reflexes that do you not one bit of good when faced with the power of Hel."

Slagfid stood, rose to his full height. Guthorm was right, of course. Probably even one of the draugar would have slain him. He could not hope to win against two, much less face the sorcerer assassin. He looked to where his sword lay a dozen feet from him, beyond Guthorm. It might as well have been on the other side of the sea.

"I do not fear my death." A lie. Guthorm's threat to raise him as a draug hung about his neck like an anchor, a chain wresting all hope from him.

"You should. Only darkness remains for you."

Slagfid roared a battlecry and charged forward. He would die a warrior. He leapt into the air, throwing his whole weight behind his descending knife. Guthorm's blade bit deep. Slagfid felt it cut through his spine.

He did not feel himself hit the ground.

Darkness shrouded him, as Guthorm had promised, and the Niflung prince snickered. Slagfid could not move, could only stare up at the vile sorcerer. He was dead. His body broken, his mind unable to escape it. All color, all light began to seep from the World.

Guthorm wiped his hands in Slagfid's blood and began to trace strange runes on the ground, on rocks, even on the twisted tree.

The World flickered and darkness swallowed everything.

And then there was light. A thousand colors of it, painting the sky. A star-filled sky, unobscured by mist. And a figure drifted toward him, winged, a faint radiance wafting off her.

Guthorm had become but a shadow, his words a senseless whisper. He was cursing the woman, trying to banish her.

Svanhit smiled down at him, reached a hand toward his hand. And Slagfid stepped out of his corpse. He stood beside his wife whole, if not alive. The world around him pulsed, the ground gave way, and a profound vertigo forced him to shut his eyes.

When he opened them, Svanhit still held his hand. They stood upon a rainbow that stretched infinitely in both directions.

"Wife?" His voice rang oddly in his own ears.

The valkyrie stroked his cheek before shaking her head.

"You came for me."

"Of course I did."

Slagfid looked around. Starlight and colors and a world

with no horizon, no beginning, no end. Something between death and whatever lay beyond. "You stopped him from taking my soul."

"Yes. You will not serve the Niflungar, nor face torment from the Queen of Mist."

"Then we can be together."

Now she shook her head once again, eyes filled with none of her usual joviality. "I can only take you to the threshold. Where you go now, I cannot follow."

"No." He shook his head. "Then take me back to Midgard, or stay here with me."

"If I returned you to Midgard, you would become a ghost even if the Niflungar did not bind you to their will. Either way, you wouldn't like it." She winked, though it seemed forced and brought no smile to his face. She sighed. "Nor can we stay here. This is a Realm for journeys. It is not a destination. Your destination is ahead, Slagfid."

Slagfid stared up at the strange, starry sky, unsure even what to say. He had so many questions. What had happened to Volund and Agilaz? What would he find at the end of this journey and why could Svanhit not join him? And, had he ... "Will the others, will Kelda make it?"

"Yes, it seems she will. Thanks to you."

He opened his mouth to ask further questions.

Svanhit forestalled him, pressing a finger to her lips, kissing it, then pressing it onto his. "Shhh. I am not permitted to give you any more answers." She pointed in one direction. "There lies the Mortal Realm and your eternal damnation." She turned, pointing the other way. "There, you will find the light. But I loved you, so I will not force the choice upon you. Go where you wish, prince who once was mine."

A beat of her brown wings carried her high into the sky.

He watched her long after her form had disappeared beyond the stars.

If the valkyries spoke of their mistress at all, it was with some mix of reverence and fear. If he went where she had bid him, he would no doubt find that mistress and she would decide his urd for him. If he turned back ... There was naught left for him. He deluded himself to think he could ever see anyone he cared for again. Volund, Agilaz, even Kelda. They were gone from him.

But his wife had come for him, spared him that damnation. And in the end, his trust in her was all he had left. Because the unknown future might still be better than the torment waiting behind him.

And so he walked toward the light.

PART III

Year 98, Age of Vingethor
End of Summer

25

AGILAZ

"So now you're human too, mama?" Hermod asked.

They had agreed to return to Vestborg. After all Volund had done, there was no going back to his brother. It weighed heavy upon him when Olrun had told him Slagfid had died, fallen in battle. She knew, for he had died gloriously and thus been chosen by the valkyries. An urd Agilaz had expected for himself. And it would have been, had a mother not so loved her child. Though he liked to think he carried as strong a weight in Olrun's decision.

"More so than you, most likely."

Though she spoke lightly, her words felt heavy to Agilaz. They had spoken of it once, when Hermod was born. That she, not quite human, might have passed on some of that nature to their child. Never had he demonstrated any such tendency, but then, he was young. No one who knew the truth of Volund's lineage could deny what impact it had had upon him.

"But why?" Hermod asked. "I liked your wings."

Olrun laughed, but her eyes looked sad. "So did I. But a

valkyrie cannot make as fine a wife for your father as a woman can."

"Oh." Hermod walked in silence a while longer. They moved through the forests nigh to Halfhaugr, and hoped to pass the night within the safety of its walls. A few nights, maybe, if Hadding favored them.

Soon, the first flakes of snow would fall. Winter loomed again, and he was eager to be settled for it, to find a warm hearth and claim some quiet with his family. Slagfid had said they would all meet again after one year. That year had passed, but Agilaz would not return to Wolf Lake. If he was to have a home now, it would be among the Hasdingi.

First, though, they needed to see Hadding, to be certain the jarl still wished Agilaz's service at Vestborg. He had left with Hadding's blessing, but things could change. Especially if word had reached them of Nidud's falling out with Agilaz.

Word had already outpaced them on one story, though Agilaz did not know if it were truth. But skalds already sang of the cruel smith Volund, and of the fallen king Nidud. In the end, they claimed, the king had hung himself from the platform. Ordered his body not be removed until ravens had eaten the last of his flesh. It sounded more like a skald's fanciful end to the morbid tale, but who could say? Agilaz's beloved little brother had become a legend, not only for his skill, but for the depths of his unmatched revenge against the tyrant king. There was a horrid poetry in that, though Agilaz could only pray no one came to associate his name with Volund's. Such ties were now a great liability to the family he had left.

"So," Hermod asked finally, "weren't you a woman before, mama?"

She chuckled. "Ask your father."

"Papa?"

"We will discuss it when you are older."

"Why?"

Agilaz was spared having to answer that by the sound of footsteps in the forest ahead. He held up a hand, stilling his son, then crept forward, while readying his bow. Hasding scouts, most likely, but he could not be too careful. As predicted, war now raged between the Hasdingi and the Skalduns, and had even begun to spread to other tribes. The chaos was like to go on several summers unless something changed, though men already spoke of Jarl Borr of the Wodanar trying to bring peace.

No scouts were here, though. Instead, Hadding crouched by a small creek. The jarl set a wrapped baby down in the woods and rose, shaking his head. Exposing the child.

Agilaz cleared his throat, and Hadding spun, hand on his sword hilt.

The jarl groaned then. "I had begun to think you'd not return."

"The child is deformed?"

Hadding shook his head. "No. She's beautiful, perfect. But Liv didn't survive the birth, and Fjorgyn won't have the girl in our hall."

Agilaz slung the bow back over his shoulder. That explained a great deal. "Liv was not carrying Erik's child at all. It was yours."

The jarl shrugged and spread his hands. "And if another man had so abased his wife, I might have had him hanged. But my wife has agreed to keep it quiet so long as the child is gone. What would you have me do, man? If I keep her, I shall never hear the end of it."

Twigs crunched behind him. Olrun and Hermod. How much had they heard?

"You found your wife."

"Yes."

Olrun's eyes darted to the baby. Finally, she nodded.

Agilaz sighed. Urd was odd, twisted. Or maybe the gods had a sense of humor not so different from Slagfid's. "I was fond of Erik and Liv both, despite what happened."

"So were we all."

"My wife and I would be honored to foster this child."

Hadding shuddered and at once swept the babe up in his arms. He stared at her for a long time before finally approaching and handing the babe to Olrun. Agilaz's wife took the child without comment, but her smile was warm.

"She has milk?" Hadding asked.

That earned him a scowl from Olrun that might have sent other men shitting themselves. "We'll manage," Agilaz answered before Olrun decided to unleash her anger. "The girl has more chance to survive on goat's milk than she does on water from the creek."

Hadding hung his head. "You shame me."

"No, you honor us."

"You won't earn gratitude from my wife for this, you know."

Agilaz looked at Olrun, cradling the babe, and to Hermod, now peeking at his new sister's face. "I don't care."

"Well, in either event, you have *my* gratitude. You have saved me from making a terrible mistake. I will never forget what you've done, Agilaz Wadeson."

"Just Agilaz, now. I make my future among the Hasdingi. Myself, and my family."

"Then Vestborg is yours, my friend." Hadding turned to go.

"What is her name?" Agilaz called after him.

"You saved her life," Hadding said. "Fitting you should decide."

Agilaz looked to his wife, who smiled down at the babe. "Sigyn," Olrun said. "Our little victory."

The girl was staring intently at Olrun, eyes with startling intelligence. Sudden, unnamable emotion forced Agilaz to steady himself against a tree. He had lost his brothers forever. But he had not only regained his wife, they made themselves a full family with a proper home.

As they walked, Olrun began to sing to the babe.

However twisted urd might prove, he had much to be grateful for.

26

VOLUND

As a raven, Volund could cover vast stretches of ground in a single night. He could not stand the sight of the sun, of course. It burned him, as it burned all svartalfar. When daylight approached, he would fly to one ruin or another, take shelter from the painful rays. Shadows would well around him then, soothing and counseling, obeying his whims as need be.

Perhaps he could not walk well. He could, however, fly. And so he passed the nights, flying from one battlefield to another. Ravens were a common enough sight in such places. They feasted upon the slain. But then, so too did valkyries flock to the fallen. And now, he could see them whether they willed it or no.

They never knew him for what he was, of course. If they had, perhaps they would have struck at him or shunned him or even fled. But they ignored him, and he watched. Waited. He had seen Svanhit once, but he did not reveal himself. Even if she knew where her sister was, she was not like to reveal it willingly. And Volund meant her no harm. Svanhit had never wronged him, and thus he could hardly visit ill upon her.

And svartalfar visited ill upon all who saw them. That was what Altvir had held back in him until, after nine wondrous years, she could no longer deny her oath. And when she had left, the darkness had wakened from its long slumber. Nidud, the fool king, could not have imagined he imprisoned not only a prince, but a dark alf waiting to rise. Soldiers spoke of the king the night before his last. In his despair, he had cast himself from his own platform, howling as he hung there, long in dying. And Volund had not made good on his threat to carry Nidud's soul to Hel. Somehow, though, he suspected the king would find his way to the Queen of Niflheim.

Volund hoped Queen Ragnhild would *not* be too quick to join her late husband. Let her suffer the loss of her children. Let her wither in grief, dwindling through the remaining years of her life, knowing her grandchild would be Volund's spawn. Altvir had warned him his seed might carry on this darkness. Now it seemed fitting.

He flew over another battlefield. This battle had raged well into the evening. Otwin, the eldest and last remaining son of Nidud, continued his father's campaigns. Given the recent events in his house, Volund suspected his rule would not be an easy one. Some claimed the gods cursed Otwin's line. It was not far from the truth. Volund, after all, was no longer a mere mortal. And he had weighed the idea of hunting down this Otwin. But the last son was naught to him, and if Nidud was dead, the king had naught else to lose.

He alighted on a withered tree atop a hill, one giving him a clear view of the carnage.

A handful of valkyries lurked about, drifting among the

dead and dying. Only those on the very edge of death could see them. A man's eyes lit in fear and longing and, sometimes, the barest hint of hope just before the end. To Volund, it seemed the valkyries pulled an Etheric light from the slain and carried it away with them.

Such was the true duty of valkyries.

The World of Dark called to Volund. It was the destination of the most wretched of the fallen. Those driven mad by hatred, unable to let go and destined to become one with the dark. Others, the weak and cowardly, would probably fall into Niflheim. And the glorious dead ... wherever the valkyries took them was a place beyond his reach. If Valhalla existed, he would never see it.

He was a vaettr, and he might enter Svartalfheim. He could, were he so inclined, then cross over into Niflheim or other adjacent worlds. He could not, however, enter the World of Sun, if that was where the valkyries went. Whatever power to which Altvir and her sisters answered was beyond his reach.

In this Realm, though, he was unusual. He had become his own host and, as such, might walk freely in the Mortal Realm as so very few vaettir could do. Walk figuratively, if not literally.

The nearest valkyrie woke him from his musings. She was looking at him. Altvir. Had he found her at last or had she chosen to finally reveal herself? It mattered not. A beat of his wings carried him to her and, as he touched the ground, he melted like a shadow and rose up as a man. An ashen-skinned, ebon-haired man, but at least he bore the semblance of a mortal. It was something.

Altvir swallowed hard. Her hand lay on her now-bulging belly.

Volund sputtered, all his constantly rehearsed lines

dying on his tongue. Whatever he had thought to say to her, to hear from her, he was not prepared for this.

"Volund." Altvir shook her head sadly.

"I ... found you."

"You lost me." Her voice was barely a whisper.

Volund swallowed, reached for her, but she flinched away. "Is that my child?"

"You sired two sons. I don't think either will ever truly be your child." Her eyes welled with tears for the second time in all their years together.

"Two sons ... twins?"

"No." Altvir looked away. "One son I gave you in the last days before my oath forced me from your side. A dream I wanted to share with you, if I could. And one son you got on the princess of Njarar. So that you might be born again in pain and live in shadow."

Bodvild, of course. But how did Altvir even know about that? Volund shook his head. "I had no choice. Vengeance demanded I ..."

"You always had a choice, Volund. You could have remained at Wolf Lake, waited for me."

"W-waited! You abandoned me with naught but a ring with which to find you." He held up his hand where the now-black ring rested upon his little finger once again. "I tracked you with it and they dared take it from me. It lost its power because of what they did to us."

She shut her eyes, and a single tear fell down each cheek. "It lost the power because of what you did to yourself, Volund. I gave that to you in the hopes you would cling to the light until I could return. The ring was a mirror of your humanity, and you cast it aside as surely as if you had destroyed the ring itself."

Volund forced his trembling hand to his side. "You have no idea what they did to me."

"I know what they did to you. And I know what you did to them. And that was your choice. You chose to descend into a dark place where I cannot follow."

What was she saying? He had finally found her again. All of this, he had done only for her. To hear such judgment, such condemnation, was an insult to all he suffered and fought for. He reached for her hand again, and she fell back, shaking her head.

"There is no future for us, Volund. Even if I gave up who I am, there is no turning back from where you have gone. Your choices are few now. Eternity alone, or else seek the company of your own dark people."

"No. No! You give up too easily. I am not broken, I am *tempered*. I have become strong."

"So strong you cannot stand the light of the rising sun. And it will rise soon, dark smith. Best you find a hole to hide in before that." Her voice broke at the last. Before he could speak further, she raised the hood of her cloak and became a swan, instantly taking flight off to the east. Toward the rising sun.

Where she knew he could not follow. Could never follow.

Volund slipped to his knees. And he roared at the fading night.

The other valkyries turned and stared, some making warding signs, others backing away. Even the Etheric souls, ghosts they drew forth, watched him in horror. He was like a wraith. Damned to wander in torment, ever mourning his losses and hateful of those who retained what had been stolen from him.

He laughed without humor. And then, as a raven he flew.

To the north rose mountains, and within them caves. Any would do to hide from a single sunrise. But Volund needed to hide from every sunrise until the dying of the World. And so he took the deepest paths, as one trained in Nidavellir knew how. Deep paths which would lead to tenuous borders between the Mortal Realm and the Other-worlds—into the World of Dark.

They were waiting for him, he knew. He could feel it. His people waiting for their great smith to come. With every step he grew more certain of it.

There was no light left for him in the World.

And so, one last time, he descended into darkness.

THE CYCLE CONTINUES ...

Next Book: Centuries before the time of Volund, the Old Kingdoms destroyed one another in their brutal wars. Audr, last Prince of the Lofdar, would do anything to save his people and his son ... no matter the cost to his soul.

The Son of Nott: books2read.com/mlnott

Join the Skalds' Tribe newsletter and get access to exclusive insider information and your FREE copy of *The Moments of Kadmus*.

https://www.mattlarkinbooks.com/skalds/

ABOUT THE AUTHOR

Matt Larkin writes retellings of mythology as dark, gritty fantasy. His passions of myths, philosophy, and history inform his series. He strives to combine gut-wrenching action with thought-provoking ideas and culturally resonant stories.

Matt's mythic fantasy takes place in the Eschaton Cycle universe, a world—as the name implies—of cyclical apocalypses. Each series can be read alone in any order, but they weave together to form a greater tapestry.

Learn more at mattlarkinbooks.com or connect with Matt through his fan group, the Skalds' Tribe:

https://www.mattlarkinbooks.com/skalds/

AUTHOR'S NOTE

Darkness Forged takes place twenty years before *The Apples of Idunn* (the first book in *The* Gods of the *Ragnarok Era* series). *Darkness* recounts the beginning of the Njarar War, as well as the birth of Sigyn, one of the main characters throughout the series. Here, also, we can see how Odin's father, Borr, would come into a situation in which a leader was needed to restore peace to the tribes.

The story of Volund (often called Wayland) comes from the *Poetic Edda* as well as the *Thidrekssaga*, with mentions present in other German and Old English sources as well.

Agilaz (sometimes called Egil) receives fewer stories about him, most of which are recounted in this book.

Most readers cannot help but notice the strong parallels between the legend of William Tell and story of Agilaz. The Tell story is much more familiar to most audiences, but is, in fact, a much later tale, possibly inspired by the supposed feats of Agilaz. Those interested can find this same tale recounted in *Thidrekssaga*.

Very little remains of stories about Slagfid. Consequently, his tale in *Darkness Forged* is my own creation, drawn from bits and pieces of other Norse tales.

Scholars have spent a lot of effort debating whether dvergar (dwarves) and svartalfar (black elves) and dokkalfar (dark elves) are all the same thing. Compelling arguments have been made on both sides, and I went back and forth as well. As with many creatures in Norse and Germanic mythology, the lines are rarely clear and allow for substantial overlap. For the context of a fictional world, however, one needs some kind of answer. Obviously, I finally settled on them being two distinct but related types of Otherworldly entities.

This proved to be one of the darker books I've ever done. I also think it's one of the best, and I really want to thank those who helped with it: Brenda, Sean, Fred, Hanna, and Clarissa. And as always, special thanks to Juhi.

If you liked this one, be sure to check out *The Apples of Idunn* and the rest of *Gods of the Ragnarok Era* and *Runeblade Saga* series.

Thanks for reading,
     Matt

For Juhi. You have never stopped believing in me. I could not do this without you.